T₁

MW01137570

A Chocolate Centered Cozy Mystery Series

Cindy Bell

ISBN-13: 978-1535178846

ISBN-10: 1535178841

Table of Contents

Chapter One

The curtains fluttered as a strong breeze passed through them. Ally glanced up at the motion and smiled as she saw her cat, Peaches, prance across the windowsill. She reached up a paw and batted at the curtains.

"Don't you do that. Those curtains are not your enemy." Ally laughed and scooped up the cat before she could get her claws tangled in the material. Peaches nuzzled her chin with the top of her head and let out a low, frustrated meow. "I know, I know, we haven't had many adventures lately." Ally felt a pang of guilt as she carried her cat into the living room. She'd been rather busy with the chocolate shop recently and had been spending less time with Peaches and Arnold, who shared the small cottage she lived in. Although, they always had food, and exercise, it wasn't the same as spending time playing together. She pulled out a stick with a feather on a string and trailed it across the floor for Peaches to chase. The cat stared at her for a moment as if she was offended, then pounced on the feather. Ally grinned.

"See, you're never too old to play."

Arnold, her grandmother's pot-bellied pig, lumbered out of his bed and snorted as the cat bounced around the living room. "Look at her go, Arnold, isn't it great?"

Arnold stuck his snout in the air and grunted. "I know, I know, you want to go for a walk." She glanced at her watch. "I have a little time before I have to meet Mee-Maw. I suppose we can take a little walk." She grabbed Arnold's collar and leash. As she stepped outside she noticed several of her neighbors were out on the sidewalks. Many walked in the same direction. She knew exactly where they were headed. Emma's yard sale.

By the time noon rolled around she and her grandmother would deliver some tasty treats for people to enjoy, but the early birds couldn't wait to dig through the treasures spread out on folding tables. Ally was just as excited. She had known Emma when she was growing up, but because Emma was about ten years older than Ally they had never really been friends. When Ally had moved back home to the small town of Blue River to live with her grandmother after a messy divorce and she had met Emma again, Ally had taken an immediate liking to her.

Emma was a regular at 'Charlotte's Chocolate Heaven'. She would often come in for a coffee and chocolate treat after her shift as a nurse at the hospital in the neighboring town of Mainbry. She and Ally had become quite friendly. They would stop to have a conversation and if Ally had the time they would have a coffee together. They shared a love of cats so they would often talk about them. Emma enjoyed talking about her two cats especially since her ex had taken them when she remarried because her new husband didn't want them in the house. Ally wasn't sure why, maybe he was allergic to them.

Emma had become known around town as

the ultimate collector. She didn't collect just one type of thing, she collected many things, and usually resold them for quite a profit. Now and then her home would become overrun with trinkets and souvenirs and that was when she would plan a big sale.

"Morning Violet." Ally smiled and waved to the woman across the street from her.

"Morning Ally, morning Arnold." Violet waved back, but continued to hurry along. Everyone wanted to be first at the sale. The more Ally thought about it, the more tempted she was to rush right over and take a look herself. But she knew that her grandmother would be waiting at the chocolate shop to prepare the brownies, and Arnold wouldn't like his walk cut short. Ally decided to take the street that was one street further away than the one she usually took so she would avoid some of the people rushing to the sale.

As Ally rounded the block to head back in the direction of the cottage she noticed some overgrown bushes in front of one of her neighbor's houses. The mailbox was also stuffed full. She paused at the end of the driveway and peered towards the large front window. The house was dark and quiet. There was no car in the driveway, but in the small town some people didn't drive cars. Ally had never met the occupant, but from gossip around town she knew that an elderly lady lived there. She had lived there for the few years when Ally lived in the city. The woman had only moved back into the house a few weeks ago after spending many months living with her children after her husband had passed away. Perhaps she had moved to her children's house again or was on a long vacation. The woman was known as being unfriendly, but how bad could she be. Ally lingered there for a moment as she tried to decide what to do. Arnold decided for her and began to waddle up the driveway.

"You're right, Arnold, it's better to be sure." She walked up to the front door and raised her hand to knock. However, before she could land a single knuckle, the door swung open.

"What are you doing on my property?" The woman barked out her words and held a broom in her hand. "Take that ugly swine away from here."

"I'm so sorry, it's just that your mailbox is full and I thought maybe..."

"You thought I was dead, huh?" She clucked her tongue and waved the broom above her head. "You wish. Then everybody could throw a party. No, I'm just fine. I don't want any of that mail. It's full of bad news. So, get on out of here before I decide to have bacon for breakfast." She gnashed her teeth in Arnold's direction. Arnold squealed and backed away.

"Stop, you're scaring him." Ally put one hand on her hip. "There's no need to be so upset. We're leaving."

"Good riddance." She slammed the front door. Ally jumped at the sound.

"Well, people weren't exaggerating, she certainly isn't the friendliest, is she?" Ally raised an eyebrow and led Arnold away from the door. On the way back to the cottage she thought about whether she anticipated ever being that surly. Perhaps aging created a sense of bitterness for some people. Or maybe it was more of a brain chemistry issue. Either way she decided she would keep an eye out for the woman. After she dropped Arnold off she headed to the shop. It did not surprise her that her grandmother beat her there and already had the first batter mixed.

"Is there still time for me to help?" Ally offered a guilty smile. "I got a little distracted on my walk with Arnold."

"There's plenty of time." She handed her a small tasting spoon. "This is just the test batter. The next one will be for Emma. Taste."

Ally dipped the spoon into the batter and tasted a small amount. "Mm, this is delicious."

"Yes, it is, but the next one will be even better. You get started on it while I get this one in the oven."

Ally snatched an apron from the hook beside

the counter, then she washed her hands in the nearby sink. Once they were dry she began putting together the ingredients for her grandmother's secret recipe. It was really only secret because she changed it every single time she used it. She would bake a batch of brownies with the current base recipe, then add a new splash of something or alter the measurements. By the time Ally had most of the batter prepared her grandmother was back by her side.

"Here are the chopped pecans," Charlotte said as she handed her a bowl of the nuts.

"Yum!"

"Add a bit more milk chocolate." Charlotte nudged her with an elbow as she looked over her shoulder.

"Are you sure? There's already quite a bit."

"These have to be the best brownies ever."

"You say that about all the brownies we make." Ally laughed and added some more chocolate pieces.

"It's true, every time." Charlotte picked up a spoon and slowly stirred the mix. "If we don't constantly strive for the best then someone else will beat us to it."

"I'm pretty sure we're the only chocolate shop in town." Ally winked at her.

"Right now we might be, but you never know how things will change. Besides, you can never add too much chocolate."

"That's not true, remember?" Ally laughed.

"Oh yes, how could I forget? The chocolate volcano of fifth grade."

"It wasn't really my fault." Ally's eyes widened. "Can you blame the curiosity of a blossoming mind?"

"Yes, I absolutely can. I told you not to add the whole bottle."

"But I wanted it to look very real. Anyone can make a little spurt, I wanted to wipe out the entire island." She picked up the bowl and began to smooth the batter into the waiting dish.

"It was quite real when it splattered over the entire fifth grade class, and even more real when I got the phone call from the principal."

"At least it was tasty." Ally grinned as she slid the dish into the oven. "No one can complain about that."

"I had to pay for new outfits for all of your classmates."

"I had to scrub the floors, walls, and even the ceiling."

"I helped you with the ceiling."

"I remember." She turned to face her grandmother. "You were so angry, but you made sure to tell me that I'd made the best volcano in the history of the school."

"Because you did. Nothing wrong with giving credit where credit is due." She winked at her. "Besides, I had the best laugh when I saw that crotchety, old teacher of yours with chocolate all over her. She was always snippy with me."

"I didn't know that!"

"Well, I couldn't exactly congratulate you. I had to be your mentor."

"You still are." Ally gave her a quick hug. "I'm so lucky to have you, Mee-Maw."

"And I you, Ally. Never forget that. Life is unpredictable and best spent with the ones that you love." She raised an eyebrow. "If you know what I mean."

"Luke?"

"Luke."

"He's busy, Mee-Maw."

"No one is ever too busy for the people they care about. Don't let excuses get in your way."

"I hear you." Ally sighed and set the timer on the oven. "These should be ready in about twenty-five minutes."

"Do you have those boxes of chocolates ready for the yard sale?"

"Yes, they're on the counter by the fridge," Ally said. "I'll go get them and load them into the van."

"Thanks Ally."

Ally picked up the boxes and took them out to the delivery van. She glanced at her watch. The yard sale would be in full swing.

Once the van was loaded she headed back into the shop. As she walked into the back she noticed that the scent of the brownies baking already filled the air. The scent drew forth memories of many occasions throughout her childhood. Brownies were as common as vegetables on her plate.

"Let me get this cleaned up so we can be ready to go," Ally said.

"Excited about the yard sale are you?"

"You wouldn't believe how many early birds I passed on Arnold's walk." She shook her head. "We'll be lucky if there's an empty hanger left."

"Don't worry, most people don't know real treasure from junk. There will be plenty to sort through."

Ally sank her hands deep into the soapy water

and washed up the bowls and utensils. By the time she was done, the brownies were done. Charlotte stowed the first batch for their own supply then wrapped up the second to take to Emma.

Ally walked out the back and put the brownies in the back of the van.

"I hope she will like the brownies," Charlotte said as Ally got into the driving seat.

"I think it's sweet that you still worry about whether people will like your brownies. You know everyone loves them."

"I still hope every time." Charlotte patted her knee. "You never know when someone's taste can change, or when the same recipe just isn't good enough anymore and people try other things."

"Excuse me?" Ally laughed as she looked over at her. "Does that have a double meaning?"

"All I'm saying is that those who drag their feet end up alone."

"That's pretty blatant."

"It's my truth." Charlotte waved her hand

through the air.

"That's not true, you're one of the most popular people in town. Besides, I'm sure Mrs. Cale, Mrs. Bing and Mrs. White would love to spend more time with you."

"Don't start with those ladies. They gossip so much it makes my head spin. Don't get me wrong I like them, but I don't think I'd fit in."

"No, you probably wouldn't." Ally smiled.

Chapter Two

When Ally and Charlotte arrived at the sale it was tough to find a spot to park. Ally finally managed to squeeze in-between a truck and a van. Ally noticed how busy the sale was. Even if the early birds had already picked it over, there was clearly plenty left to sort through. Although Emma's sales were always large, this time it seemed even bigger. Ally and Charlotte placed the chocolates and brownies on one of the tables with a sign indicating that they were complimentary. They also left some menus and cards next to the boxes. They found that providing some treats for free helped generate new business as well as create a positive image of the shop. It was a very valuable marketing tool.

"I'll start at this end." Charlotte headed for the other end of the tables while Ally started at the first table. There were many conversations buzzing around her, but she zeroed in on the objects on the table. Yard sales were always fun, because she would imagine what the items were used for, and how valuable they were. Old toys always gave her a pang of nostalgia for her own childhood. Some items were so well worn that it was clear they were extra-loved. Sometimes she would buy something just because it deserved to have a nice safe home on a shelf. However, she learned to curb her buying habits when she ended up with no shelf space.

As Ally looked through the tables the crowds began to dwindle. Several of the tables were covered with various sports equipment, from ballet shoes to tennis rackets. Emma always found a way to keep herself busy and active. Ally rummaged through a pile of costume jewelry. Her grandmother was right, it was easy to find treasure when you took the time to look. As she pulled apart necklaces she heard Emma's voice raise.

"You can't do anything about this. The house is in my name, and I'm ready to move on."

"You know as well as I do that I paid for at

least half of that house. Not only that but I painted it, I fixed the stairs, I even redid the basement. You're going to tell me that I have no say in what happens to it?"

"No, you don't. I got the house in the divorce, and that means I have the right to sell it."

"Fine, then sell it to me."

Ally glanced up and caught sight of a lumbering man that stood in front of Emma. He was at least two feet taller than her and had to be close to three hundred pounds. The way he glared at her made Ally think that he was accustomed to intimidating Emma. Ally presumed it was her ex as she knew that Emma had divorced and remarried just over a year ago. Ally decided to walk over just in case things got any uglier.

"Gary, you can't afford it and you know it. I can't take a loss on the house just to make you happy."

"Yeah, there were a lot of things that you couldn't do just to make me happy. Don't you want the cats to have a proper home?"

"Of course I do, Gary. I appreciate that you took them for me, but they will be happy wherever you live."

"I'm telling you right now, I'm going to fight you on this. I'm not going to just let some stranger live in the home that was supposed to be ours."

"Whatever you think is going to happen, isn't. You don't have any control over this, or me anymore, Gary. Now, just go before I have to call the police."

"Oh sure, call the police." He scowled at her. "Fine, I'll go. But this is mine." He grabbed an old, ragged set of golf clubs and turned around. He almost walked straight into Ally, but she stepped out of the way just in time. He grunted and stormed past her. Ally tried not to laugh as a few golf balls fell through a hole in the bottom of the torn bag.

"Are you okay, Emma?" Ally looked over at the woman. Her cheeks were red, and her lips were tight, but she appeared calm enough.

"He just likes to make a scene. He always did.

Any kind of attention he can get, he'll get."

"I'm sorry about that."

"Me too." She sighed. "Like anyone was going to buy those golf clubs anyway."

"I didn't know you were selling the house. Is this the final yard sale then?"

"Yes, it is. I haven't made it too known as I wanted to avoid a run-in with Gary. I want to be more mobile. As you know my new husband, Jack, is an over-the-road trucker. I've recently decided that I'd like to get an RV and be able to meet him at different places so we can spend more time together."

"That's a wonderful idea. I hate to see you leave though."

"Oh, I'm sure I'll be back to visit. I love this town. I mean I grew up here. Remember I mentioned how the community rallied around me when Gary and I got a divorce? I've never felt more supported."

"I remember." Ally nodded. "And just know

that you still do have our support."

"Thanks Ally, that means a lot."

"We left some brownies and chocolates on the tables like we usually do."

"Oh yum, thank you." Emma smiled. "Did you find anything you liked?"

"I'm still looking." Ally smiled at her.

"Okay, let me know if you have any questions about anything. It looks like I need to talk to a man about a canoe." She laughed as she walked over to a man that had already climbed into the canoe. Ally glanced over her shoulder and scanned the remaining people for her grandmother. Before she could spot her, a squeal carried through the air. Ally laughed as she recognized it and walked towards her grandmother.

"What did you find?"

"It's for you, a keyring." Charlotte held up the keyring to show her. It was a colorful butterfly decorated with fake gemstones.

"That's pretty," Ally said as she took it from her grandmother to look at it closely.

"Oh, look at this!" Charlotte picked up a wooden box. It had beautiful patterns carved into it. "The patterns are so intricate." She ran her fingertips along the etchings in the wood and gazed at it with affection. She opened it up and looked inside. There was nothing in it. It was shallow with a thick base. "It will be perfect for storing bits and pieces." Charlotte had a love of trinkets and wooden statues and decorated the shop with them. She mostly bought ones made by local artists. "I would love to add this to my collection. Emma, do you know anything about this piece?" She walked over to show it to her. Emma glanced at it, but was distracted by people who had just walked up to the sale.

"I don't know, I found it with some junk in the basement and put it out here. You can have it for five dollars if you want."

"Five? Sold!" She smiled. "Ally has the cash." Ally glanced up from the pan she considered buying.

"I do?"

"Yes, you do. Don't you?" Charlotte raised an eyebrow.

"Oh right, I do." She reached into her pocket and pulled out money for the wooden box, the keyring and the pan. After she paid she put her keys on the keyring. As she did she noticed that the colorful stones were sparkling in the sun. Then she decided to look around a little more to see if anything else caught her eye. Suddenly, a cloth flower appeared before her eyes. It seemed to hover in the air for a moment before she noticed the hand that held it. She smiled as she followed the arm to a familiar face.

"Luke, you made it. I didn't know if you would have time to stop by."

"I wasn't sure if I would, but I'm glad I did. Emma has some great stuff."

"Yes, she does. Did you spot anything you liked?"

"I have my eye on a few records, and of course, I helped myself to a brownie or two. Delicious, as always." He gazed into her eyes.

"Don't worry I kept some extra for you." Ally smiled sweetly and poked him in the stomach. "Can't let you go hungry."

"Thank you, thank you, thank you!" He grinned and kissed her cheek. "How could I be so lucky?"

"Just because I bake you brownies?"

"Just because you're you." He brushed a strand of her brown hair back behind her ear and leaned in a little closer. "Can I see you tonight?"

"For dinner?"

"I have to work late. Maybe dessert?"

"Sure, I think I can make that happen. My place or yours?"

"Yours, if you don't mind. I'm in the middle of a project at my place that might just take me a year to finish. I don't know how I convinced myself that I could redo my own floors."

"You can, you're just a little busy. I could help you if you would like."

"I'm sure that's not how you want to spend your free time."

"As long as it's with you, I'll enjoy it."

"Hm, I like that answer." He wrapped his arms around her waist and drew her in for a quick kiss.

"Ally! Look what I found!" Charlotte's shrill voice pulled them apart. Ally laughed and shook her head.

"She's in heaven."

"I bet. I have to get going, but I'll let you know what time I'll be getting off tonight, okay?"

"Sure. It doesn't matter though. No time is too late."

He smiled at her again, then walked off. Ally watched him go, though pretended to be digging through an assortment of gardening supplies. She couldn't help but smile to herself at just how handsome he was. She remembered the first time she met him, and how uncertain she was of his intentions. It didn't take long for her to recognize that he might just be the best man she'd ever met. But, was Gary the best man that Emma ever met before things went south? Did all romantic ties tear people apart?

Chapter Three

Later that day Ally spent some extra play time with Peaches and Arnold. Though she managed to get them both into a game of tug of war, one with a piece of string, the other with a thick rope, she couldn't enjoy it as much as they were. Her mind drifted back to the way that Gary had raised his voice at Emma. There was such cruelty in his tone. She wondered how Emma really handled it. It was so difficult to deal with the drama of an ex. Though they weren't very close friends Ally thought they could be with a little effort. She decided to make her another batch of brownies to take over.

As she mixed the batch she considered what it would be like to be confronted with her own ex. It felt like such a long time since things fell apart between them and she had moved back to her grandmother's cottage, that she barely even thought of him anymore. But if he showed up out of the blue, she would have a few choice words for him. As she poured the batter into the pan to put in the oven, her thoughts returned to those first few days after the break-up when she believed that her heart would never stop aching. Now, she barely recalled feeling that way. In fact, she was more interested in what she felt about Luke than she was in what she felt about some ex-husband from the past. With so much to look forward to, she didn't feel a need to dwell on the past. However, she still felt uncertain about what exactly the future was going to bring.

When the brownies were finished she set them on the counter to cool. Then did a quick clean-up of the baking tools that she had used. She cut the brownies into squares and placed them in a small glass dish that was decorated with flowers. It made them look even more appealing. She made sure that Peaches and Arnold had plenty of food and water, then headed out with the brownies. It was easy to think that everyone had it hard, and Emma's situation wasn't unique, but Ally could tell from the conversations they had

had that she was the type of person who cared about everyone and didn't like to see anyone's feelings get hurt. Ally thought that it must have been upsetting for her that her ex-husband was so upset, and her new husband was too far away to comfort her.

Ally drove the few blocks to Emma's house and parked out front, where the tables for the yard sale were set up earlier that day. She noticed that one of the tables was still up, but empty. She glanced back at it, then walked up the front steps and knocked on the door. After a few minutes with no response she knocked again. Again, there was no response. Emma's car was in the driveway. Was she just not in the mood for company? Ally thought it was a bit rude not to at least open the door and tell her that. She decided to call her, since she wanted to deliver the brownies, and didn't want to leave them on the doorstep. The phone rang. As it rang in her ear, it also rang inside the house. She held her breath and put her ear to the door. It sounded as if it wasn't far from the door. Why would Emma be hiding inside and not answering the door or the phone? Ally tried to think of whether she'd said anything that could have offended her when she had seen her at the yard sale. She'd barely said anything at all. She was just about to turn and walk away when she decided to make one last attempt at getting Emma to answer the door.

"Emma? It's me, Ally. I brought you some more brownies. I just want you to know that I'm here if you want to talk." Her mind raced with crazy ideas. Had Gary returned and gotten her so upset that she didn't want to talk? Was she perhaps in a part of the house that she couldn't hear the door and it was just her phone that was by the door? She knocked harder. She waited. Still the door did not budge. Then it struck her that the house was quite dark inside. From what she could see there were no lights on in the living room, the front hall, or any of the upstairs windows. Her heart sunk. What if Emma was hurt? That might explain why there was one table still left out front.

Ally reached out and tried the knob of the front door. If it was locked, she would go home, if it was open, she would at least check on her. It turned without resistance. Her stomach churned. If Emma was avoiding her, and she just burst right through the door, what would the woman think of her? As her heart raced and her mind whirled with potential explanations she pushed the door open. She had no idea what she expected to find. However, as the door glided midway open she noticed a pair of sock-covered feet lying on the floor. In that brief instant she became aware that something was terribly wrong. Her heart dropped as she stepped inside. There at the bottom of the stairs was Emma's body.

"Emma!" Ally's purse and the brownies slipped from her hands as she rushed towards her. The glass container shattered when it hit the tile floor. She barely even heard the noise as she pressed her fingertips against the side of Emma's neck. Ally's eyes filled with tears as she realized that Emma was dead. Ally started to panic and was in a bit of a daze. Through the fog she realized that she needed to call for help. She crunched glass shards under her shoes as she grabbed her purse and pulled out her phone.

Ally went through the motions of requesting help, her voice unsteady and her mind unaware of what was or wasn't said. As her senses began to awaken from the shock of what she had found, she heard police sirens in the distance.

Ally's naturally curious mind couldn't resist trying to put the pieces together. Emma stood at the top of the stairs. Did she hear something? See someone? Why did she go down the stairs? She closed her eyes and tried to imagine it. Then there was the fall. Did it start at the top of the stairs or did it happen further down? She noticed that she had socks on her feet and the stairs were wooden. Maybe she moved too fast. Maybe she just slipped.

The front door burst open and two paramedics rushed in. Ally stepped back, and though she knew there was nothing that they could do, she still hoped. Not far behind the paramedics were two police officers, and right behind them, Luke walked in. He looked from Emma's body, to Ally.

"Ally, what happened?"

"I don't know. I was going to deliver her some brownies, and she didn't answer, and the door was unlocked." Her voice trembled. "I can't figure out how this happened. She was already at the bottom of the stairs when I got here."

"Looks like she's been dead for some time. The medical examiner will have to declare an exact time," Luke said.

"The yard sale ended four hours ago." She bit into her bottom lip. "What if I had just come back earlier? Maybe there would have been a chance to help her."

"Not with these injuries." The paramedic shook his head. "I've never seen such a severe blow to the head from a fall down the stairs."

"What could cause such a hard blow?" Ally

stepped closer to the paramedic.

"Ally, we shouldn't try to jump to any conclusions, the medical examiner will know better than any of us," Luke said to her, but he stared at the paramedic.

"He's right about that." The paramedic nodded. "I don't have the training to figure any of that out, I'm just speaking from my own experience, which isn't much. I shouldn't have said anything at all."

"Do you have any ideas though?" She looked back up the stairs.

"I shouldn't." He looked from her to Luke, then back again. "I'd better get to my report." As he walked away Ally frowned and turned back to look at Luke.

"He obviously thinks that something suspicious happened. He was afraid to speak in front of you."

"I don't think that's the case at all. But really, he should have been more careful about what he said. It's not his place to define a death or injury. That's up to the medical examiner."

"Yes, I understand that, but something feels off about all of this and he obviously thinks that the injury was caused by something other than just falling down the stairs. Emma was a very athletic woman. She played sports, she was active. I'm sure she'd been up and down these stairs millions of times. I know it's possible, but I find it hard to believe that she would just lose her balance or forget a step."

Luke looked up the stairs. "The steps aren't very wide."

"But they don't curve, there's no strange turn to them." She shook her head.

"Accidents happen. Everyone makes mistakes, Ally. Sometimes you turn the wrong way, or the phone rings and you look up at the wrong moment."

"So, you're just going to write it off as an accident?" She looked into his eyes. "Are you sure about that?"

"I'm not sure about anything. My first instinct is that it's accidental just from looking at the scene. Because we can't be certain the medical examiner will have a look at the body, then we'll know for sure. I try to reserve my judgments until all of the evidence is evaluated."

"Why would she leave the door unlocked?" Ally asked.

"Maybe she came in for something and was on her way back out. She slipped. Or perhaps she had a heart issue from all of the labor throughout the day. Maybe she was a little confused and exhausted and she just slipped."

"She did leave a table up outside, which I thought was odd. But she is wearing socks. If she was headed back out for the table then where are her shoes?"

"Maybe she didn't want to dirty the house." He pointed to a pair of grubby sneakers by the front door. "It looks like she just kicked them off."

"You're right." She studied the scattered shoes. "But still, I don't know." Ally frowned. "It doesn't seem right to me. She's lived in this house a long time. I'm sure she knew how to be cautious on the stairs."

He cupped her cheeks and looked into her eyes. "We will just have to wait and see, Ally, there is no way to know right now."

"Yes, I guess there isn't." She sighed. "I'd better call Mee-Maw before she finds out from someone else."

"I'm going to wait here for the medical examiner. I'll let you know as soon as I find anything out. All right?"

"Yes." She squeezed his hand. "Thanks."

"Anytime." He glanced at the other officers, then leaned close and kissed her cheek. "I'll stop in after I'm finished here."

"Okay, that would be nice."

As Ally left the house her stomach churned with dread. She dialed her grandmother's number and rehearsed in her mind how she would break the news. Her grandmother picked up on the first ring.

"Ally, I just heard! Is it true that you're the one who found her?"

As Ally's mind swirled with emotions all she mumbled was an apology. "I'm sorry, I broke the dish that the brownies were in."

"Ally, please don't apologize. Do you want me to come to you? Are you okay?"

"No, it's fine, Luke will stop by when he's done at her house. At the moment he thinks it was an accident."

"Is that what you think?"

"I'm not sure. Maybe I just want there to be more of an explanation to it than that."

"Some things just don't make sense."

"That's what Luke said."

"You trust your instincts, Ally. If you think there is more to it, then we will look into it."

"Okay, thanks," Ally said. "Do you know if she still had any family in the area?"

"I don't think so. Her mother moved to Florida and her father died a few years back. She has a sister, but I don't think she lives nearby."

"I'll try to find out what the arrangements for her will be."

"Yes, absolutely. We could offer to cater or help with the arrangements."

"Good idea, Mee-Maw."

"If you need me just call me."

"Thanks." Ally hung up the phone and wiped her eyes. As much as she wanted to think that Luke was right, and there was no reason to believe that it was anything other than an accident, she couldn't get out of her mind what the paramedic had said and she wanted to find out exactly what had happened to her.

Ally unlocked the door to the car and started to step in when she noticed a person across the street from the house. It only took her an instant to recognize her. It was the woman who had threatened her and Arnold earlier in the day. She leaned heavily on a cane and stared hard across the street. But she didn't look at the police cars, or the house, she looked right at Ally. Ally shuddered and ducked into the car. As she started it, she wondered if maybe the woman was somehow involved. She certainly seemed cruel enough. But she pushed the thought out of her mind. She was just a cranky, lonely woman who was spying on the neighbors. It wasn't surprising, considering that all of the sirens and chaos were not common in Blue River and certainly not on such a quiet street.

Chapter Four

Ally drove back to the cottage and was relieved to be greeted by Peaches the moment she opened the door. She crouched down and scooped the cat up into her arms. With one cheek buried in the cat's soft, warm fur she made her way to the couch. Arnold bounded into the room and snorted at her. He expected a snack, or a walk, but she just wanted to enjoy their company first. After a few minutes of her two pets nuzzling and soothing her she was ready to work out if there was more to Emma's death. She grabbed her phone and dialed her grandmother's number again. When she answered, Ally was even more calmed by the sound of her voice.

"I just want you to know that I'm home."

"Oh good, sweetheart. I was worried. How are you holding up?"

"I'm okay."

"I've been fielding phone calls from everyone

in town. I guess news has gotten out that you were the one to find her. Be prepared for the questions."

"I know, I know." She sighed.

"I wonder if her husband even knows yet?" Charlotte said.

"Oh my, I hadn't thought of that. I hope they were able to reach him. We should make an effort to do something nice for him."

"Yes we should, Ally. That's a great idea. Call me if you need me. Okay?"

"I will, Mee-Maw." Ally hung up the phone and closed her eyes.

As Ally began to sort through her thoughts there was a knock on the door. She walked over and opened it.

"Come on in, Luke."

Arnold walked over to the door to say hello as Luke stepped inside. Luke patted him on the head. Even though he was becoming fond of the pot-bellied pig he still looked a bit uncomfortable around him. Ally went to sit back on the couch next to Peaches.

"Hey." He offered her a mild smile as he walked towards her. "How are you doing?"

"Okay." She patted the seat next to her. Peaches lifted her head to look in his direction. She offered a soft meow, then settled her head back down on top of her paws.

"Hi Peaches." Luke stroked the top of her head. "Keeping Mom company I see. She's such a sweet cat."

"Yes, she is." She glanced over at him. "Did the medical examiner arrive already?"

"Yes. He's taken custody of the body."

"Did he mention anything about the death?"

He frowned. "He's not going to conclude anything until he does the exam."

"What about Jack? Her husband? Did anyone reach him?"

"We're trying. We're having a hard time pinning down exactly where he is at the moment.

We're still looking into it though, hopefully he'll be notified soon."

He intertwined his fingers with hers. Ally stared into his eyes for a moment, then smiled.

"You must be starving. Let me make you something to eat." She stood up and headed for the kitchen.

"Please don't go to any trouble for me." Luke followed after her.

"Peanut butter and jelly?" She picked up a butter knife and smiled.

"Sounds delicious."

"Strawberry or grape?"

"Strawberry." He leaned against the counter. She felt his eyes on her as she went through the process of making the sandwich. "I know what you're thinking."

"Whether or not I should cut the crusts off?" She glanced over at him.

"No. About Emma's death not being an accident." He leaned closer. "I like the crusts."

"You're right." She offered him the plate and then began to make her own sandwich.

"Your instincts are telling you something, it's okay to listen."

"What about your instincts?" She finished her sandwich and they sat down at the small kitchen table. "What are they telling you?"

"All I know for sure is that Emma died. The scene really didn't tell me anything else. Until we find something to indicate foul play, I really can't even investigate much more than that."

"Ah, but that's not what I asked you." She took a bite of her sandwich.

"Okay, okay. My instincts tell me that it's a little odd for a woman of her age and health to fall down the stairs. But it's not unheard of. The wound on her head could have been caused by the fall, but the paramedic seemed to think it's unlikely. I want to hear what the medical examiner says."

"Yes. I wish he would hurry up."

"Patience."

She sat back in her chair and finished her sandwich. Luke opened his mouth to speak but the front door opened before he could.

"Ally, we need to talk." Charlotte bustled right past the two of them at the kitchen table and to the stove where she started to make a pot of tea.

"Mee-Maw, what's wrong?" Ally stood up from the table with Luke right behind her. When Charlotte turned to face Ally she gasped with surprise.

"I didn't realize you had company, I'm so sorry, Ally. I thought Luke was coming over later, I didn't think he would be finished at the scene so soon. I didn't mean to intrude. I'll just see myself out."

"Nonsense." Luke shook his head and placed a hand on her shoulder. "What's going on? You seem upset."

"I am a little upset. No, I'm a lot upset." She sighed and went back to the kettle. As she set it on the stove she continued to speak. "I've been thinking about Emma, and how she had so many plans ahead of her. She was just about to move, to start a new life. After what you said, Ally, I just don't believe it was an accident."

"That's what we were just talking about, Mee-Maw. I don't really believe it was an accident, either. In my gut, I just think that something else happened. Maybe I just don't want to believe it. My gut tells me that there was someone else there with her."

"But, there's no evidence of that. No sign of forced entry, no sign of a struggle, nothing." Luke held out his hands palm up. "I've got nothing to base an investigation on." He paused and looked between them. "Well, not nothing. Your instincts mean a lot to me. But that's not enough to start an investigation."

"I can't blame you for that. I guess hunches aren't going to get you anywhere." Charlotte sighed and leaned against the counter. "So, what we need to do is get some proof. I'm sure that we can put our heads together and figure this out. There must have been something we overlooked in her life. Who would be angry enough to push her down the stairs?"

"We don't even know that she was pushed or that she fell down the stairs." Ally tapped her fingertips along the counter beside her grandmother. "Couldn't someone have just made it look like she fell down the stairs? Maybe she was killed somewhere else in the house."

"I hadn't really thought about that. But you're right, Ally." Charlotte clucked her tongue just as the kettle began to wail. She turned to take it off the burner.

Luke's cell phone began to ring. "Excuse me, ladies, I need to take this." As he stepped out onto the back porch, Ally set tea cups on the counter for her grandmother.

"I hope we're not putting too much pressure on him to agree with us." Ally frowned. "He has to keep his objectivity."

"Luke is his own man, he can trust our

instincts if he wants to."

"Do you really think that's what it is, or do you think he's trying to be nice?"

"Maybe a little of both." Charlotte tipped the kettle and poured the scalding water into the cups. The aroma of lemon and honey filled the kitchen.

"That's what worries me. I'd never want to come between Luke and his job, and I don't want what he feels about me to taint his decisions when it comes to his work."

"I don't think you have to worry about that, sweetheart. Luke knows how to figure out how to keep work and romance separate." She carried her cup of tea to the kitchen table. "Besides, even if he does lean a little more towards your view of things, your view is usually pretty spot on."

"Maybe." Ally stirred her tea. A moment later Luke stepped back into the kitchen. He didn't look at either of them as he sat down at the table.

"Everything okay?" Ally peered at him.

Charlotte nudged his cup of tea towards him.

"Sure." He nodded. "What were we talking about?"

"Hunches," Charlotte said.

"Honestly, I'm just a little amazed by your hunches. I just spoke with the medical examiner."

"And? Did he rule it an accident?" Ally scooted her chair forward.

"No, he obviously hasn't made a ruling yet because he still has a lot more examining to do, but he said at the moment it looks like it's accidental. He noted that the severity of the injuries although unusual for a fall down the stairs were still possible to be caused by it. But he can't tell conclusively, yet?"

"So, at least he hasn't made a ruling yet," Ally said.

"He can only go by the evidence that is in front of him. So far he didn't find any hairs or other trace evidence on her body that could indicate that someone harmed her. Without some kind of proof that someone else was in the house with her there's no way to prove foul play."

"What do you think, Luke?" She looked into his eyes. "Now that you've heard from the medical examiner?"

"Honestly, I expected him to rule that it was absolutely an accident. The fact that he found something that makes him hesitant, tells me a lot. I don't know if this was a murder or not, but I do think it just got a little more mysterious." He sighed and picked up his cup of tea.

Ally rested her hand on top of his. "And?"

"And, I think you might be right. I think I definitely need to look into it more while we wait for his findings as there might have been more to this death. I trust your instincts and the fact that you are so convinced it wasn't an accident tells me that I might be overlooking something."

"Oh good, thank you."

"I might have to do it on the side because I'm working a big case at the moment and I doubt my captain is going to open an official investigation before the medical examiner has made his final ruling or something else comes to light." He looked over at Ally. "Is there anything you remember from the day of the yard sale that might give me some grounds so my boss will allow me to start an investigation?"

"Yes! Maybe there is!" Ally stood up and began to pace beside the table. "Her ex-husband Gary showed up at the sale. He was livid that she was selling the house. They got into an argument right there in front of everyone."

"Okay, that might be something. Did he threaten her?"

Ally frowned. "Not exactly. But he was quite aggressive and he took some golf clubs."

"Took them?"

"He just picked them up and walked off with them. I think they were his, though."

Luke shook his head and stood up. "That's not going to give me much. Anything else you can think of? Something he might have said?"

Ally closed her eyes and thought back to the conversation. As she recalled one thing stood out to her.

"He kept saying that she couldn't sell the house. That it was his house. He was talking about how he did all of these fixes and upgrades on the house and one of the things he mentioned fixing was the stairs." Ally's eyes widened. "Do you think he might have done something to the stairs?"

"I'll see if I can find anything structurally wrong with them, maybe the railings loose and been put back in place." Luke made a note of it in his phone. "It's a place to start. I can poke around a bit." Luke rested his back against the wall and crossed his arms. "I'll see if I can find out more about him. Do you know anything that can help, Charlotte?"

"Not much." Charlotte pursed her lips and picked up the empty tea cups. She set them carefully in the sink and turned the water on to rinse them. "Just that everyone knew that their marriage ended horribly."

"When did the marriage end?" Luke asked.

"A couple of years ago. Of course I've never discussed this with her myself, but this is what I've heard. She was scared that if she got divorced she would lose the house to him so she stayed in the marriage. But then she met Jack and got the courage to leave him."

"Sounds like her knight in shining armor." Ally grabbed a towel to dry the tea cups.

"I'm definitely going to see what I can find out about this guy. But we can't open an official investigation, yet."

"Don't worry about that, Ally and I don't need a paper trail to open an investigation. Do we, Ally?"

Ally shook her head. "We have our ways. Maybe we can find you the proof that you need."

"I know it's pointless for me to tell the two of you to be careful, but remember that this is a sensitive situation involving a man that appears to be quite volatile." He reached out and pulled the towel from Ally's hand, then took her hand in his.

"I don't think that's something that any of us can forget," Ally said as she recalled the way he spoke to Emma at the yard sale. She wondered if he knew then what he intended to do. Did he plan it out beforehand? Or was her murder a spur of the moment decision?

"Hey Ally, don't worry. I'm going to have a chat with him," Luke said.

"How can you do that without opening an investigation?"

"I'll say that someone mentioned that he had a confrontation with his ex-wife at the yard sale and that I am following up on it."

"Do you think you can get away with that?" Charlotte frowned.

"I can get away with some things as long as I'm careful. There's nothing wrong with a friendly conversation."

"Fair enough." Charlotte nodded. "I just hope that it will lead to something more."

"I can assure you if he confesses to anything he'll be taken care of right away. I still need to consider this an accident, but it's worthwhile to see if he says anything to make me think otherwise."

"All right, I should probably head home. The shop is going to be hopping in the morning. Ally, you don't have to come in if you don't want to."

"No, I want to. I'll be there." She hugged her grandmother. "I'll see you then."

"Goodnight, sweetheart." Charlotte kissed Ally's cheek. On her way out she patted Arnold's head and made kissing noises and then stroked Peaches' back as she wound through her legs.

"I should go, too. I'll walk you out, Charlotte." Luke met Ally's eyes. "Are you going to be okay by yourself?"

"That's a silly question, Luke. I'm always okay by myself."

"But it never hurts to have company!" Charlotte called out before she stepped out the door. Luke met Ally's eyes one last time, then followed after Charlotte.

Ally smiled to herself as she closed the door behind them. She could pretend to be insulted, but Luke's concern meant a lot to her. As soon as she was alone the exhaustion hit her like a brick. She barely made it to her bedroom before she had to collapse. She curled up in her bed and stared at the patterns of moonlight on the wall. Her entire body felt heavy, too heavy. She thought about getting up and taking a shower, but she couldn't bring herself to crawl out from under the covers. As if she sensed her restlessness, Peaches jumped up into the bed with her. She rubbed her furry cheek along Ally's and purred.

"Thank you, Peaches. It's been a rough day." She pulled the cat close and stroked her back. As she fell asleep she thought about the events of the day.

Chapter Five

When Ally opened her eyes she felt as if she hadn't slept at all. Yet the sun was up and the clock showed that she was actually running late. She had a quick shower, dressed and took care of the pets, then headed out to the shop. When she arrived she was relieved to smell freshly baked muffins waiting for her.

"I'm here, Mee-Maw, sorry I'm running a little late."

"Don't be sorry, sweetheart. You had a big day yesterday. Just come try one of these chocolate muffins."

"If I must." Ally sighed and grinned at the same time. "They smell so good. Did you add something new?"

"Just a hint of cinnamon. I know it sounds strange with chocolate, but it just gives it a little zing. At least, that's what I'm hoping." Charlotte handed her a muffin.

Ally took a small piece off the top. "Yum! It's delicious."

The bell over the door chimed and Mrs. Cale, Mrs. White, and Mrs. Bing filed inside. Each had a solemn look on their face.

"Good morning, ladies." Ally turned to face them and offered a small smile.

"Good morning." Mrs. Bing sighed and slouched down in a chair at the counter.

"Coffee?" Charlotte patted Mrs. Bing's hand.

"Yes, please."

Ally slid the sampler tray towards the three women. "Help yourselves, ladies, we all need some comfort food today."

"Yes." Mrs. White looked at the tray deciding which one to choose. "Though I'm sure going to need a lot of those to comfort me." She popped a chocolate in her mouth.

"Does everyone around town know?"

"Yes, and they know that you were the one to find her." Mrs. White looked into her eyes.

"How did everyone find out so quickly?" Ally frowned.

"Well, it started with all of the sirens and police. Then, Mavis was standing outside the post office this morning, absolutely ranting about how Emma was murdered."

"Murdered?" Ally froze where she stood. "But the police think it was an accident."

"Yes, as do most people in the neighborhood." Mrs. Cale picked up a piece of chocolate and studied it. "But apparently Mavis believes there is more to the story."

"Who is Mavis?" Ally looked between the three women.

"She's a bit of a recluse." Mrs. White frowned. "And eccentric."

"More like crazy." Mrs. Cale laughed.

"Crazy?" Ally pursed her lips. Before Ally could ask more her grandmother walked over.

"Let's try to have a good day today. In honor of Emma, hm?" Charlotte set down a tray with cups of coffee on it, along with some of the muffins she had baked. "The muffins are on the house."

"Oh, thank you!" Mrs. White breathed in the scent of the muffins. "They smell heavenly."

"I hear that there aren't many people coming into town for the funeral." Mrs. Bing shook her head. "It's a shame that she didn't have more family."

"Well, the town will be out to support her, and Jack. That poor man." Mrs. White sighed. "So young and already a widower, it's so tragic. I'm sure he will kick himself for not being there when she died."

"Well, he wasn't gone yesterday. I saw him in the city." Mrs. Bing shrugged.

"Wait, what? Are you sure?" Ally met the woman's eyes.

"Sure as I can be. I know a handsome man when I see one. Anyway, what does it matter?" Mrs. Bing asked.

"I thought he was out of town on a run yesterday," Ally explained.

"I suppose I could be mistaken." Mrs. Bing shoved a large piece of the muffin into her mouth. Ally wanted to ask her more, but she decided against it. It would be easy enough to check and see if Jack was on his run or not the day before. She didn't want to spark even more gossip.

"I heard that Jack's back home now," Mrs. Cale said.

While the three ladies busied themselves with their coffee and muffins Ally made her way to the back room. Charlotte soon joined her.

"Did you hear what they said about that woman?" Ally began to set up more chocolates on trays.

"I did. You know Mavis. She's the one that lives in that overgrown house that you visited yesterday with Arnold. The one that doesn't like Arnold."

"Oh, that's Mavis!"

"Maybe she is just ranting and raving. She could just be a little off her rocker. I wouldn't read too much into it."

"But how would Mavis know? Maybe she's a witness. Maybe she knows something about the murder."

"Maybe, but I doubt she'll tell us anything. She certainly isn't easy to talk to and is probably just a little confused." Charlotte glanced at her watch. "After lunch let's take something over to Jack. I want to see how he's doing."

"Okay." Ally returned to the dishes. Her thoughts swirled right along with the dishwater. When her cell phone rang she jumped. She'd been so deep in thought that she forgot where she was for a moment. A quick glance at the screen told her that it was Luke.

"Good morning, Luke."

"Good morning, Ally. I wanted to reassure you that I am looking into Emma's death. I spoke with Gary this morning."

"I'm all ears." She turned off the water and leaned against the sink.

"He had no idea that Emma was dead."

"He could have been pretending."

"Maybe, but he seemed very shocked. After that I couldn't get much out of him. He insisted that they just argued at the yard sale and he dropped it after that."

"Nothing sent up a red flag for you?"

"The guy was a mess. To be honest I'm not sure what to believe about him at this point. I guess it's possible that he was faking it, but I've been doing this for some time, and he seemed genuine."

"All right, thanks for updating me, Luke."

"How are you this morning?"

"I'm doing okay. Did you hear about the woman outside the post office this morning?"

"Yes, a patrol officer took care of that. He suspected the woman heard about Emma's death and became paranoid about it."

"She didn't have any real evidence that it was a murder?"

"No, he said as soon as he arrived she stopped shouting and started mumbling about cover-ups, and the town being a hot bed of ignorant criminals."

"Wow, quite opinionated."

"Yes. Anyway, we think she might have needed some mental help which we are going to organize, but nothing to be too concerned about."

"Okay, thanks Luke. You should come by when you can, Mee-Maw made some fantastic muffins."

"First chance I get, I'll be there."

"We're closing after lunch."

"My morning is pretty packed. I'll text you if I can get over there."

"Bye Luke."

When he hung up the phone Ally sighed. One more dead end, and nothing to convince Luke that the death might be a murder. Although many customers came into the shop throughout the morning the normal jovial atmosphere wasn't there. Most people uttered a few words, or discussed in whispers what had happened to Emma. After lunch, Ally was more than eager to close up.

"I don't think I could take one more sad look in my direction." She frowned as she locked the door. "I wish so many people didn't know that it was me that found Emma."

"It's a small town, unfortunately everybody knows everything," Charlotte said.

"Yes, but I wonder about Mavis ranting near the post office this morning. Does she know more than all of us? Maybe I should try to talk to her."

"First, let's head over to Jack's. I'm sure he's had his share of casseroles brought to his door, let's bring something sweet to him," Charlotte suggested.

"Yes, I want to see how he's doing. I'll take care of closing up." Ally grabbed a rag and some cleaning solution to wipe down the counters.

Charlotte tapped her chin as she looked through the selection of chocolates. "What kind do you think Jack will like? Emma used to buy a variety. Jack only moved to Blue River when he married Emma a few months ago and was often away for work so I don't think I've ever seen him in the shop."

Ally frowned as she looked in the display case. "I'm not sure. Maybe we should just take him some of each. If he just lost his wife he may not even want to eat, so at least he'll have something to offer any guests or family members that might be there for the funeral."

"Good point. I'll put together a big box." As Charlotte set about packaging the chocolates, Ally noticed the sign for Emma's yard sale still hung in the window. With a heavy heart she walked over and took the sign down. She couldn't bring herself to crumple it up and throw it away so she folded it neatly and tucked it into the drawer under the cash register. She reached into her purse for her phone to check for texts. When she opened her purse, she noticed the wooden box that they had purchased from the yard sale.

"I guess this is even more of a treasure now, isn't it?" She held it up for her grandmother to see. Charlotte wrapped the chocolates in a deep purple bow and then looked up.

"Yes, it is. Maybe you should have it at the cottage for a while. It might not be a good idea to put it on display in the shop just yet."

"You're right. Someone could recognize it from the sale. We'll wait a few months then add it to the collection." Ally tucked the box into her purse and then took the chocolates from her grandmother. "Should we head over now?"

"Better now I think, before too many people have a chance to bother him."

"Good idea." Ally headed out the door and waited for her grandmother to walk out before she paused to lock it. As she looked through the thick glass at the shop inside, she was filled with gratitude for the wonderful memories it had given her.

Chapter Six

After the quick drive to Emma's house, Ally waited for her grandmother to join her on the sidewalk before she started up the stairs. She noticed that the table that had been left up outside, was gone. Jack likely put it away. She cringed at how difficult every little thing was going to be for him. With the house for sale, would he have to pack up their lives together? It made her sad to think that he might have to do it alone. She hoped he had family or friends that would help him. She knocked on the door and waited. Charlotte clung tightly to the box of chocolates.

"I hope he doesn't think we're too intrusive."

"I'm sure he will appreciate the gesture." Ally glanced up as the door swung open. A man she'd only seen around town a handful of times opened the door. He was exactly what many women dreamed of. He was tall, dark, handsome and looked very fit. He must have followed the same athletic lifestyle that Emma did.

"Hello, can I help you?" He looked between the two of them.

"Jack, I'm Charlotte, and this is my granddaughter, Ally. We just wanted to offer our condolences for your loss." She held out the box of chocolates. "It's not much I know, but Emma did love the chocolates from the shop."

"Thank you. Yes, she loved the chocolate shop in town. Ally, are you the one who found her?" His eyes widened. Ally nodded as tears misted her eyes. She placed her keys in her purse and fished for a tissue. She fumbled the wooden box out of the way to get to the package. When she pulled one out she dabbed at her eyes.

"Lucky you were there." He looked up from her purse and sighed. "I wasn't due to be home for three more days. I can't even imagine if no one had found her before then. I'm sorry, it must have been traumatic for you, but it means a lot that you visited her. Please, come inside." Jack gestured for the two of them to walk past him. Charlotte took Ally's hand and gave it a squeeze as they were led inside. Even though Emma's body had been removed and the broken glass from the brownie container was cleaned up, the entire scene flashed before Ally's eyes when she stepped inside. Jack led them into a small sitting room not far from the steps. "I hope you don't mind me asking, Ally, but why did you come visit her?" He gestured for them to take a seat on the couch as he sat down on a chair.

Ally sat down across from him and looked into his eyes. She held tightly to her purse on her lap as a form of comfort. "Well, after her fight with Gary I just wanted to make sure that she was okay."

"Gary was here?" He raised an eyebrow.

"Didn't the police tell you?" Charlotte shook her head. "We told them about the argument at the yard sale."

"No, they didn't tell me. All they told me was that it looks like it was a terrible accident. I guess they didn't think it was necessary to mention the fight. It's strange that Emma didn't tell me he was

70

at the sale. She knows she's supposed to let me know any time she sees him."

"Oh?" Ally frowned. "Why is that?"

"I know you're probably thinking I'm some kind of jealous fool that didn't want his wife around her ex, but that wasn't the case. Gary has a temper. I didn't like her to be alone with him, because I've never trusted him. In fact, I've come close to knocking him out myself for the way he spoke to her."

"Yes, he was quite angry at the yard sale," Ally said. "I wish I had stayed with her."

"I'm sure that even if you did you couldn't have stopped her from slipping," Jack said.

"He's right, Ally." Charlotte nodded. "There was nothing that could have been done."

Ally lowered her eyes and cleared her throat. She tried to hold back the questions that bubbled up in her mind, but she just couldn't resist.

"Is that what you think happened, Jack? I mean, can you really picture Emma slipping and falling down the stairs?"

He stared at her for a long moment. "Well, I try not to. But I suppose that's what happened. That's what the police said they think happened."

"But the medical examiner is investigating, right?"

"Ally." Charlotte placed a hand on her arm. "Take it easy, I'm sure that Jack doesn't want to think about that."

"Wait, what are you saying?" He looked between the two women with wide eyes. "Are you asking me if I think it wasn't an accident?"

"I just mean, with the argument only a few hours before, and Emma's not the type to be clumsy, is she?"

The skin on his face drained of color and he looked down at his clutched hands. "I hadn't even considered the idea that maybe it wasn't. What kind of husband am I?" His eyes filled with tears just before he squeezed them shut.

"Jack, don't you know that she was having the

yard sale so that she could sell the house? She adored you. She couldn't wait to spend more time with you. She was happy to spend the time she did with you. Please don't think that you've done anything wrong," Ally said.

"But I just agreed with the police that it was an accident."

"It may very well have been an accident." Ally bit into her bottom lip.

"It's just hard for us to believe that she died from an accident, Jack, that's all." Charlotte sighed. "We should go, Ally."

"No, wait. Please." He stood up from the couch and looked at both of them. "I think you might be right. Emma was never one to be clumsy. She's never once even missed a step on those stairs. Maybe Gary was involved somehow."

"We don't know that he was. We don't know anything at this point." Charlotte shook her head.

"All we know is that he was angry," Ally said.

"The police will look into it." Charlotte

narrowed her eyes.

"What if they don't?" Jack's lips parted in shock. "What if they just assume it's an accident and never look into Gary at all?"

"If there is something to find, I'm sure the police will find it. Now, we really should be going, Jack. If you need any help with the funeral, or any guests that are coming in for the funeral, please let us know," Charlotte said.

"The funeral," he murmured and collapsed back down on the couch. "I hadn't thought too much about that."

"Do you have family that can come help you during this time?" Ally offered a sympathetic frown.

"No. I don't have any family."

"None?" Charlotte raised an eyebrow. "No close friends?"

"No. No one." He covered his face with his hands. "I don't need anyone. I can handle it. Thank you again for the candy."

"If you need anything, don't hesitate to call," Ally said.

He mumbled something and nodded. As she followed her grandmother out the door Ally found it hard not to go back to Jack and offer to stay. He seemed so alone, and there was no one to comfort him.

"That was hard." Ally frowned as she opened the car door for her grandmother.

"Yes, very. He's going to be grieving for a very long time."

The drive home towards Charlotte's apartment was a quiet one. Ally tried to let go of the idea that Emma was murdered. When she stopped at the retirement community Freely Lakes, Charlotte looked over at her.

"I have some chocolate cookies I made last night. Would you like to take some home? It looks like you need some cheering up."

"I'd love some." Ally smiled as she opened the car door. "How did you have the time to make those?"

"There's always time to bake."

"Thanks Mee-Maw."

"I hope you understand why I stopped you in there." Charlotte looked over at Ally.

"I am always certain that you have your reasons. I know that before we went you were just as suspicious of Gary as I was."

"And I still am. But I don't want to upset Jack any more than he already is. We need to be careful how much we say. What if we're wrong? What if it was an accident? Or maybe it wasn't, but Gary had nothing to do with it?"

"I never really thought that far ahead. I was hoping that Jack would give us some information that would help us figure things out," Ally said as they reached the door to Charlotte's apartment.

"So was I, but we may have to wait until he has a chance to adjust to the news." Charlotte reached into her purse to get her keys.

"Good idea. I'll get the door." Ally used the

spare keys she had on her keyring to open the door to the apartment.

"Here are the cookies." Charlotte took a small container of cookies off the counter and handed them to Ally.

"Yum," Ally smiled as she took them from her. She gave her grandmother a warm hug. "I'll see you in the morning at the shop. Love you."

"Love you, too." Charlotte closed the apartment door.

When Ally got into the car she took out a cookie and took a bite. She immediately relaxed as she tasted the cookie. The rich chocolate was enough to sooth her nerves.

Ally started the car, then began to head back to the cottage. During the drive she noticed that everyone in town seemed to be somber. The news spread fast, and there wasn't the usual weekend cheer of children playing, yard work, or dog walking.

Ally parked at the cottage and was greeted by

a cacophony of animal sounds. After she settled Arnold and Peaches down she collapsed onto the couch. As exhausted as she was there was no way she could close her eyes. She kept thinking of Emma. As much as she believed that it wasn't an accident, she still had no way to prove that. Her cell phone rang, disrupting her thoughts.

"Hello?"

"Ally, it's Mrs. White."

"Hi Mrs. White, how are you?"

"Oh, just devastated. I don't know what to think about poor Emma. So young, and now she's gone."

"Yes, it is terrible."

"Are you all right, sweetie? We didn't get much of a chance to talk at the shop today with those two bitties gossiping." Ally smiled to herself as it was more like three bitties gossiping.

"Thank you for asking. I'm okay."

"All I can think about is her poor husband. He was gone so much, and now she's gone. He barely had the chance to know her."

"It is very sad, Mrs. White. I'm sure he'll appreciate your support at the funeral."

"I will be there. Good night, Ally."

"Good night, Mrs. White." Ally hung up the phone and closed her eyes.

As soon as they opened the shop the next morning she knew that Mrs. White, Mrs. Bing, and Mrs. Cale would be there to greet them. She knew that they would have many more questions about Emma that she had no answers to.

"Come here, Peaches, it's been a long day." Ally patted her knee. The cat jumped right up into her lap. Peaches yawned and then rested her head on Ally's knee. "So, what do you think? Can a woman with the grace of a cat end up at the bottom of a flight of stairs?" She sighed and looked up at the ceiling. "I know it's possible, I just don't think that's what happened. Emma would have fought. She would have reached for the banister, or grabbed at the steps. She would have done something to try to save her own life. I really think that the only way she fell down those stairs was if someone surprised her and pushed her or as the paramedic seemed to believe someone hit her over the head."

Peaches flicked her tail up high enough to swat Ally on the nose. She purred when Ally ran her hand along the fur on her back.

"You're right, I'm not thinking clearly. I'm too emotional because I knew Emma." Peaches purred and stretched out in her lap. "I know, I know, I can't settle down either." She glanced at her watch. It was still early enough to take Arnold for a walk. "Arnold, are you up for a stroll?" Peaches jumped to the other side of the couch. Arnold came bounding into the living room when he heard his name. He nuzzled Ally's shin as she rummaged around for the collar and leash. Once she had Arnold ready he lunged towards the front door. Ally couldn't help but smile at the strength of the small pig.

As soon as the fresh air hit her lungs some of the tension in her body eased. Maybe that was what she needed all along, a fresh perspective. Arnold seemed very interested in the grass and sidewalk. He sniffed everywhere as they walked. When they turned on to the next block Arnold's demeanor changed. He pulled her along with more force than usual. She noticed that he had a certain direction he wanted to take. As she let him take the lead he trotted right past an overstuffed mailbox.

"I told you, keep that pig away from here!"

The voice from just beside her made Ally jump. She turned to see the cranky woman step out from behind a tree.

"We're on the sidewalk. We have a right to be here."

"I don't think this neighborhood is zoned for farm animals. What's next? A rooster?" She scowled. "As if there isn't enough noise and chaos around here."

"I find it to be a fairly quiet area." Ally studied her for a moment. It was easy to write her off as an unpleasant person, but she wondered what might have made her that way. Ally wanted to ask her about what she had been heard saying by the post office, but she didn't think she would talk to her about it without gaining her trust first. Ally was also worried about her, she wanted to know that the woman was all right. "Ma'am, are you okay? Do you need help with anything?"

"Am I okay? Like I'm some feeble-minded beggar?" She glared at Ally with such an intensity that Ally took a step back.

"I didn't mean anything by it, I just wanted to make sure that you were cared for."

"Because having some nosy person to check in on you is so very important?" She rolled her eyes. "Look here, young lady, you're the one that's lost your mind if you didn't hear that ruckus last night."

"Ruckus?" Ally blinked. All of a sudden Ally recalled seeing the woman across the street after she found Emma's body. And she was the one who said it was a murder outside the post office. Ally's heart dropped. Could Mavis have been involved?

"Did you hear or see something last night?"

"Before all of the sirens?" Mavis laughed, though it sounded more like a cackle. "Everyone's in a tizzy about someone falling down the stairs. They're talking about buying safety guards and special shoes to keep from slipping. So blind, so very blind, they are."

Ally tightened her grip on Arnold's leash. "What are you talking about? You were overheard saying it was a murder at the post office. Do you know something about Emma's death?"

"Don't you, pretty lady?"

For the first time Ally looked into the strange woman's eyes. They were a clear blue so crisp that Ally was lost in them for a moment. As wild as she acted, the woman's eyes revealed a sense of confidence and peace that surprised her.

"I don't know what you mean."

"Sure you do. I saw you there, just like you saw me. We're the type that know things, aren't we?"

"Were you inside Emma's house? Did she invite you in?"

"Ah, I see. Maybe I was wrong. Just as blind as the rest. Off with you and your foul pig." She turned and made her way back towards the house. Ally stared after her. She considered following her and trying to get more information, but she was certain the woman would not be forthcoming. She decided that no matter what, she had to find out more about her. Clearly she knew more about Emma's death than she was willing to reveal. She wanted to know the woman's full name. She could ask her grandmother if she knew it, but as she looked at the packed mailbox she had an idea. She glanced around to see if anyone was around. Once she was sure that no one watched her, she plucked one of the pieces of mail out of the mailbox and read the name that it was addressed to.

'Mavis Mauder.' She tucked the envelope back into the mailbox and looked up towards the house. Ally couldn't be certain, but she thought she saw a curtain flutter. As Ally led Arnold back to the cottage she couldn't stop thinking about Mavis, and what she said. 'We're the type that know things, aren't we?' Was that supposed to mean that she and Ally were the same in some way? As soon as she was inside she headed straight for her computer. She ran a search on her name without knowing what she expected to find.

Mavis Mauder. She pursed her lips as she read through the information she could find about her. She soon discovered much of what she already knew. Mavis was eighty-eight, recently widowed, with four children. She lived alone in the house, which she owned. She wasn't able to find out much more about her. She decided that when they opened the shop the next morning, she would find out what she could from Mrs. White, Mrs. Bing, and Mrs. Cale. If anyone knew anything about the woman's history, they would. She spent the rest of the evening playing with Peaches and soothing Arnold, who still had his feelings hurt.

Chapter Seven

The next morning Ally took some time to fold and put away laundry. She had a few extra minutes when she was done. Only then did it occur to her that Luke never made it to the shop for a muffin. She decided to head to the shop early and make up a small basket to take to him. It wouldn't be something that he expected, but she hoped he would like it.

As Ally walked up to the door of the shop her mind was focused on what basket she would use and how many muffins she would fill it with. Would he be embarrassed if she carried it into the station to give it to him? Out of habit she slid the key into the lock. However, before she could turn it the door pushed all the way open on its own. Her heart stopped. Was her grandmother already there and left the front door unlocked? Did they forget to lock up the day before? She was sure they didn't. Both she and her grandmother were very careful about things like that. However, the door was open. As she pushed it open further it crunched over glass and bumped into things. Her eyes widened when she saw the debris scattered across the floor.

"Oh no! Oh no!"

"Ally? What's wrong?" Her grandmother walked up behind her.

"Mee-Maw, someone's broken in." She grabbed her grandmother's hand. "They've ransacked the place. I'm calling Luke. Her hand trembled as she pulled her phone out of her purse. "We have to find out who did this and fast."

"Wait Ally, let's take a look around." Charlotte pushed past her further into the shop. Ally followed after her.

"I'll check the back." Ally rushed past her towards the back room. As she did she heard a strange sound. It was a tune she recognized, she couldn't place it, but thought that it was maybe from a movie. But there was no television in the shop, and although she played music sometimes when she worked in the kitchen, she always turned it off before she left. So, what was making that sound?

All at once it struck her that it sounded like a ringtone from a cell phone. Whoever broke into the shop was still there. She broke into a run straight through the door that led to the back room. As she burst through it she saw the back door swing shut. As panic and fury washed over her she slammed her way through the back door and out into the parking lot. The only vehicles in the parking lot were her car and the delivery van for the shop. There was no sign of anyone else around. She spun around slowly in an attempt to figure out in which direction the burglar went. There was no sign of anyone nearby.

"Ally! I've called Luke! Did you see who it was?"

"No Mee-Maw, I'm sorry." She tried to even out her rapid breaths. "I wasn't fast enough. I didn't see anyone."

"It's all right, honey." Charlotte rubbed her upper back and patted it a little. "I'm just glad that you're safe. You shouldn't have taken off after them like that."

"No, you shouldn't have." Luke jogged to a stop beside them. "I was on my way here when your grandmother called. You didn't see them at all, Ally?"

"No." She tried to catch her breath. "I tried to catch up with them, but I just couldn't."

"It's okay. We're going to find out who did this," Luke said.

Ally took a deep breath and did her best to calm down. Luke always managed to cut through her panic. "I know, it's just that whoever it was, they were right there, and I just couldn't get there fast enough."

"I'm glad you didn't." He placed both of his hands on her shoulders. "What if the person was armed? What if they came after you?"

"Luke, you have to stop worrying about me so much. I can handle myself."

"No." His grasp tightened just a little on her

shoulders and he held her gaze. "You can't handle it. A criminal about to be caught can be very desperate and will do anything to escape. You should have called me the moment that you opened the door."

"I was going to."

"She was." Charlotte frowned as she stepped up to both of them. "I told her not to. I wanted to check out the shop before she did."

"Why?" Luke glanced over at her.

"I don't know. I guess I wanted to make sense of it, and see if anything was missing."

"All right." Luke sighed and gave Ally's shoulders a comforting squeeze before releasing them. "Let's just take a walk through together. Do you have any idea who might have done this?"

"No." Charlotte shook her head as the three of them walked back into the shop. "I can't even imagine who would want to harm the shop, or us."

"What about anyone strange hanging around? Any drifters or people you didn't recognize?" Luke paused in the middle of the front of the shop. He glanced around at the shelves along the walls.

"No one. Right Ally?" Charlotte looked over at her.

"No one that I've noticed." Ally reached down and picked up one of the wooden carvings that was in the middle of a pile of glass. "They shattered the display case. Luckily we took everything out yesterday before we left."

"It looks like they knocked almost everything onto the floor. Ally, walk me through what happened when you got here this morning." He gestured to the front door. "Was the door locked?"

"No, it was open." Ally shook her head. "I put the key in the lock, and then realized that the door was already open."

Luke walked over to it and put on a glove. He carefully pulled the door open without touching the handle. He crouched down and looked at the lock and catch. "There's no sign of forced entry that I can see. Did you leave it open yesterday?"

"No." Ally shook her head. "I thought about that, but I'm sure we locked it. I always double check."

"You were in a rush to leave right? Distracted by thoughts of Emma and going to visit Jack?"

"Well yes, but still, we locked the door."

"Charlotte?" Luke looked over at her. "Are you as sure as Ally?"

"Yes, of course." She narrowed her eyes. "If Ally says that it was locked, then it was locked."

"Interesting." He straightened up. "This door is very difficult to break through without leaving a mark," he said thoughtfully. "So, if they didn't break in, and the door wasn't left unlocked, then maybe they had a key."

"That's impossible. We're between delivery drivers right now, so Ally and I are the only ones who have a key."

"And where are they?" Luke looked from Charlotte to Ally.

"I have mine." Ally lifted her keys into the air.

"I have the key for the delivery driver on here as well."

"I have mine, too, of course." Charlotte rummaged through her purse. She paused after a few moments, then rummaged again. "Oh, I must have left it at home. Maybe." She furrowed a brow.

"So, we could have a missing key?" Luke frowned. "You need to change the locks, just in case. I'm going to get a crime scene unit over here to dust for prints. Don't clean up until then, I know it's hard, but if things are left where they are, it's for the best."

"I don't even know what they would want to steal. We don't keep more than fifty dollars in the register at night." Charlotte wrung her hands. "This is just awful. We certainly can't open up today."

"Don't worry, Mee-Maw, we'll get it all straightened out. Let's check the register and the equipment in the kitchen. That can be sold for quite a bit of money."

"Okay."

"I'll stay with you until the patrol officers arrive." Luke slipped his hand into Ally's. "I'm sorry this happened."

"I was going to make you a basket." She frowned.

"Oh?" He smiled. "That's very thoughtful of you."

"Is it? I didn't know if you would like it."

"Absolutely."

"Let me see if there are still muffins in the back."

"Thank you, but I think you're going to have to get rid of everything. Just to be on the safe side. We don't know what the person touched."

"Oh, of course." Ally nodded. "I'll just go see what we have to get rid of." She walked away from Luke and into the backroom, still in a daze. As she opened the refrigerator she noticed that her hands shook. It was hard for her to believe that the shop she'd grown up in, had been overturned by someone. She looked in the refrigerator and then at the dry ingredients. Although she was pretty sure that nothing had been touched she knew that she would have to get rid of it. She was relieved to find that there wasn't much made and they didn't have a large stock of raw products as they were expecting a delivery tomorrow. When she stepped back out into the main area of the shop she found Luke speaking to two officers.

"I want the whole place searched. I want to know who was in here, understand? Don't skip over anything. As soon as you have a name, you report it to me first." He looked between the two men. "Got it?"

Ally suppressed a smile at Luke's protectiveness.

"Yes sir. We'll get started right away."

"I hate to leave you like this, but I have to get back to the other case I'm working on," Luke said as he walked over to her.

"It's okay, Luke. I know that you're only a phone call away." Ally watched him as he walked out the door. "Mee-Maw, we should step out while the officers do their job. No need for us to hover."

"You're right." Charlotte held open the back door for her. "I want to talk to you about something."

As soon as they were outside Ally turned to face her. "What is it?"

"I think I know who did this."

"You do?" Ally's eyes widened. "Who?"

"I think it must have been Gary."

"Gary? Emma's ex-husband? Why do you think that?"

"Luke questioned him yesterday. We were at the yard sale when he argued with Emma. Remember he almost ran straight into you when he was leaving. Maybe he worked out that it was us that told Luke about the argument. Maybe he wanted to get revenge."

"Wow, I didn't even think about that. You might be right. I should let Luke know."

"No, don't. It's just a feeling I have so let's not take up more of Luke's time. I want to find out for ourselves. If Luke pays him another visit he might get spooked and we will never find out what happened."

"Well, I can get his address pretty easily. What's your plan?"

"We're going to talk to him ourselves."

"Do you think that's wise? I'm not sure that he's the approachable type."

"He doesn't have to be. He just needs to answer a few questions for us. Let him try to push me around, and he'll find out that it's impossible." Charlotte straightened the collar of her blouse. "Someone broke into my shop, our shop, and vandalized it. I'm not going to let that go by without finding out who did it. Get his address. Let's go."

Ally searched Gary's name to find his address, then followed her grandmother to her car. "It's not too far, I'm sure we can find it." As she opened the door to the driver's side she thought about the potential risk that existed. If Gary could ruthlessly murder his ex-wife he could harm anyone. As brave as her grandmother was, she also knew that sometimes she let her bravery get her into dangerous situations, not unlike her granddaughter. "Mee-Maw, maybe we should take a look around Emma's house first and see if there's any indication it wasn't an accident and if there is any evidence."

"Around, or inside?" Charlotte glanced at her.

"Inside. I bet she still keeps a key under the flower pot in the back. She told us about it when we dropped off a chocolate delivery for her and she wasn't home. Remember?"

"Oh yes, of course."

"If it's there we can let ourselves in without doing anything too risky. If Jack isn't home, it shouldn't be a problem."

"All right, let's swing by there first."

Chapter Eight

Ally turned down the road that led to Emma's house. She stopped a few houses down so as not to draw too much attention to herself. She pulled her keys out of the ignition and stepped out of the car. "Let's see what we can find, but remember to be careful. We have no idea who ransacked the shop. It could be related to Emma's death. We have no idea where the burglar might strike next."

"Let's make it a quiet entry." Charlotte nodded.

Ally led her grandmother through the small gate that led to a patch of backyard. She moved up the steps as silently as she could and peeked under a small flower pot. As she suspected the key was there. Her stomach twisted. Did Gary know that, too? Was that how he let himself into the house? She reached into her purse and pulled out a tissue. As she plucked the key from the ground she was careful not to leave any fingerprints on it.

"He could come home at any time, we need to make this quick."

"Yes, we do." Charlotte glanced over her shoulder. "Hurry."

Ally nodded and unlocked the door, then pushed it slowly open. She held her breath as she waited for someone to come charging towards her.

After no one barreled down the hall Ally took a step inside the house. The stillness of it was unsettling. No one was there to explain why the tile was pried up in the corner of the kitchen. No one pointed out the hall closet where she could hang her jacket or leave her purse. Instead, her muffled footsteps were all that filled her ears. She glanced back as her grandmother started to follow after her.

"Mee-Maw, don't you think it would be better if you waited by the door? Then you can tell me if anyone comes."

"All right, but be careful, Ally. I don't want to have to explain any of this to Luke."

"Thanks for your concern." Ally flashed her a smile then shook her head. She continued down the hall out of the kitchen and into the living room. Everything was just as it had been the day before. Not a cushion out of place. Why would anyone want to leave such a beautiful home? Maybe Emma hoped that she would finally be able to evade Gary. Maybe that was enough reason for her to pull up her roots and move on. She paused in the living room and checked under the couch cushions. She looked inside the drawers in the desk in the corner. She opened the doors of a large wooden cabinet and discovered a television, along with other electronics. Nothing out of the ordinary.

As Ally walked back towards the stairs she tried not to think about what she'd seen that fateful night. She climbed the stairs two at a time and headed for the master bedroom. Once inside she discovered that it was not as tidy. The blanket was crumpled on the floor. Pillows were strewn about. The contents of the closet had been emptied out onto the floor. With everything scattered about it looked similar to the shop. Had someone been searching through Jack's house, too?

Ally started to pick through the clothes that were scattered on the floor. It was hard to overlook the fact that she dug through dresses and blouses that Emma once wore. Underneath the clothes were shoe boxes, opened and emptied. On a hunch she walked over to the dresser and checked the jewelry box. There were plenty of necklaces and rings inside. It wasn't obvious that anything had been taken. Downstairs was immaculate. Why would someone only search the bedroom? She turned towards the bed and decided to look underneath. But as she crouched down to take a look her cell phone rang. She didn't have to check it to know that it was her grandmother, as she hung up after the first ring. That was the signal for her to get out of the house. Her heart started to race. Was Jack back?

Ally ran to the bedroom window that

overlooked the driveway just in time to see Jack step out of his car and head towards the front door. This was it. She was going to be caught, and Luke would be notified of her arrest. She could only hope that her grandmother was back at the car and driving away. She had to think fast to get out of the bedroom and down the stairs without Jack seeing her.

Already, she could hear the key in the lock and the sound of the door as it swung open. Then she couldn't, because her heart pounded so hard in her ears that she couldn't hear anything else. She heard the stairs creak, one by one, as he ascended them. Minutes, that's all she had, or mere seconds if she didn't find a hiding place. The only place she had to go was the bathroom. She jerked the door open and ducked inside. Once inside she ran to the window. When she looked out she realized it was far too high for her to climb down from. She heard Jack in the bedroom. Without a second thought she climbed into the bathtub and pulled the shower curtain enough to hide her frame. If he would just go back downstairs without going into the bathroom, she would be fine. However, as she listened she suspected he headed in her direction. She kept waiting for the moment when he would cry out, or call the police, in reaction to the state of his bedroom. Instead he ventured towards the bathroom door.

Any second Ally was sure he would discover her. She held her breath, afraid that she would cough or cry out when he walked through the door. Just as he stepped onto the tile floor of the bathroom she heard the doorbell ring. Her eyes squeezed shut as she continued to hold her breath. She didn't want to suddenly gasp for air as she was sure that would draw his attention. He hesitated as if he might ignore the doorbell. But it rang again. He turned and walked out of the bathroom. She gulped down air, but didn't give herself time to feel relief. She had to get down the stairs and to the back door without him seeing. When she heard him open the front door she rushed towards the stairs. She paused just out of sight and waited.

"Jack, I'm so sorry to bother you, I know that you're going through so much."

"It's no bother. What can I help you with, Charlotte?"

"It's Ally's car. I was just on my way into town, and it just conked out right by your driveway. I would have gone to someone else for help, but I saw you pull in, so I thought I'd take a chance."

"I can take a look at it if you want. I don't know that much about cars, but maybe I can get it running for you."

"Oh, thank you so much. It's not too much trouble?"

"It's fine. Let's just take a look at it." He followed Charlotte out through the door towards the driveway. Ally seized the opportunity and started to race down the stairs. However, when she got to the third step her shoe tilted forward and she lost her footing. With one hand on the railing she was able to catch herself before she slipped. The shock that rippled through her in reaction to almost falling was so potent that she nearly cried out, which would have surely drawn Jack's attention. The thought that immediately entered her head was whether they were wrong, had Emma just slipped? She ran to the back door and froze near the hedge when she heard the hood of the car slam shut.

"I don't see any problems. Maybe you should try starting it again."

"Okay, I'll do that." Charlotte looked towards the house then got into the driver's seat. She turned the keys in the ignition and the engine roared to life. "Wow! You must have done something!" She smiled as she stuck her head out the window.

"No, I don't think so. I just looked at it." He leaned against the window frame. "I guess it's working now though."

Charlotte nodded and smiled. "Thanks so much. I appreciate it."

"Sure, I guess." He smiled in return and waved to her as he walked back towards the house. Ally waited until she heard the front door close, then she ran to the car. She ducked down as she crawled into the passenger side.

"Go, Mee-Maw, get us out of here." She had just pulled the door shut as her grandmother pulled away from the curb and began to drive.

"Are you okay?" Charlotte glanced over at her then looked back through the windshield. "I was so worried about you."

"I'm okay thanks to you. If you hadn't drawn him out he would have caught me. Who knows what would have happened then."

"Don't even think about it. Did you find anything?"

"Not really. Other than the fact that the bedroom was torn apart. I thought that someone must have ransacked it. But when Jack walked in, he didn't react to it. It wasn't a surprise to him."

"You think he ransacked his own bedroom?"

"I think he must have. He didn't call the police, or question what happened."

"Maybe he experienced a surge of grief that drove him to do it. People grieve in different ways. He might have become overwhelmed with the reminders of Emma hanging in the closet."

"Maybe." Ally sighed and rested her head against the window.

"Or maybe he already knew it was ransacked so it wasn't a surprise to him. Maybe he just hasn't tidied it up, yet."

"That's possible." Ally nodded. "The rest of the house was immaculate from what I could see. But I didn't have too much time to look around."

"Yes, he pulled into the driveway very fast. I'm sorry that I couldn't give you more time to get out."

"Mee-Maw, don't be sorry. You protected me." Ally leaned her head back against the seat and sighed again. "That was way too close. Could you imagine if he'd caught me?" She stared out through the windshield. "Let's head over to Gary's and see what we can find out."

"I'm already going in that direction. But are you sure that you're up for it, Ally?"

"I am. I'll be fine by the time we get there."

Ally did her best to settle her nerves on the drive to Gary's house. However, the more she thought about Jack's room being a mess, and him not even reacting, the more it bothered her. Why would he tear apart the closet and throw his wife's clothes on the floor? It didn't seem like a normal reaction of grief to her. Maybe he was looking for something. But even if he was it seemed odd to her that he would make such a mess and not clean it up after.

Chapter Nine

Ally sighed as Charlotte turned the car down the road that led to Gary's apartment.

"Do you think he'll be home?" Ally asked.

"Maybe. I don't know. Do you remember what he drove?"

"A white truck."

"Okay, we can keep our eyes peeled for it. Here we are." Charlotte turned into the parking lot of the apartment complex and parked a few spaces away from the space assigned to Gary's apartment. It was empty, but Ally knew better than to believe that meant it was safe. Jack's driveway had been empty, too.

"Let's wait a few minutes and make sure he hasn't just run to the store."

"Good idea. Are you sure you want to do this? We can always come back tomorrow," Charlotte suggested.

"No, I want to do it now. I want to find out if he's the one that made the shop into such a mess. The thing that I don't understand is, how did he get a key? I know I didn't leave that door unlocked."

"I'll have to check for my keys when we are done here. We can go to my place and I'll make sure I have mine," Charlotte said.

"You're always so careful, I'm sure that you have them."

"Everyone makes mistakes now and then. You let me into my apartment yesterday. Remember?"

"Yes," Ally said.

"And I don't use the key to lock my front door, I press the button so it's locked from the inside then pull it closed." Charlotte glanced in the rearview mirror. "I don't see anyone coming this way."

"All right, let's go ahead and take a look." Ally stepped out of the car. She slid sunglasses on in an attempt to hide her features. Charlotte stepped out of the car and joined her. She was wearing a large sunhat. If someone spotted them they didn't want them to be able to give a good description.

"Let's take those stairs." She pointed to the stairs that would lead to the second floor. Ally climbed the stairs behind her grandmother and paid attention to each concrete step. "This place looks rather seedy. Let's stay close together."

When they got to the door Ally knocked. When there was no reply she knocked again. Again there was no reply. Both she and her grandmother put on gloves.

Charlotte reached into her purse and pulled out a small nail file. "Keep a lookout."

Ally nodded and watched for anyone approaching the apartment. Every shadow, every car that drove past, made her heartbeat quicken.

"What are you doing?"

"I'm picking the lock. I saw it on TV." Charlotte smiled. Ally's mouth fell open as she looked at her grandmother.

"It's clear. Take your time, Mee-Maw," Ally said as she looked up and down the corridor again.

"I don't need it, we're in." Charlotte tucked the file back into her purse.

"That was fast! How did you manage that?"

"I'm just that good." Charlotte winked at her, then shrugged. "Actually, it's open." She pushed the door open. "I didn't have to pick the lock."

"I wonder why he would leave his door open. It could be a trap. Let me go in first."

"Actually, I don't think so." Charlotte pointed to the empty apartment. "I think he left it open because he's not intending to come back."

"Well, what's a clearer sign of guilt than running?" Ally inched past her grandmother to step inside. "If he left in such a hurry he might have left something behind. We should still take a look around."

"Good idea. I'm right behind you."

Ally looked through the living room and the

kitchen. Every drawer, every shelf, was completely empty. Gary might have left in a rush, but he had taken the time to make sure that he didn't leave anything behind.

"I don't think that we're going to find anything. It looks like he tried not to leave a trace behind."

"I wouldn't be so sure. I've never known a man to be spotless."

"Mee-Maw, that's sexist."

"Excuse me?" She raised an eyebrow. "I'm just speaking from my own limited experience. I don't think it would hurt to scour every corner."

"I'll check the bedroom." Ally left her grandmother and walked into the bedroom. It was not much bigger than a closet, and there was a stripped-down bed against the wall in the corner. Ally crouched down and looked under the bed. She found nothing but dust. She lifted the mattress off the frame and peered under it. There wasn't anything to find but an old coffee stain. She set the mattress back down and looked around. A wire stuck out of the wall in the opposite corner. The small window had the shade pulled down. As she walked towards it the shade rolled up with a loud snap. She jumped at the sound and a cry escaped her lips.

"Ally? Are you okay?" Charlotte burst through the door into the room. "I heard you scream."

"I'm sorry, I didn't mean to scare you. The shade rolled up and it startled me." She walked towards the window to pull the shade back down. When she reached for it she noticed a piece of paper on the windowsill. She picked it up. "She was mine first." Her eyes widened as she read the words out loud.

"Let me see that." Charlotte held out her hand. Ally placed the note in her grandmother's hand. "As I said, they always leave something behind. I wonder if he meant to leave this behind in Emma's house."

"Why else would he write a note like this? It seems like a threat to me." Ally peered at it. "It is torn, like part of it is missing. There's nothing else on the windowsill."

"Maybe he thought he grabbed the whole note, but a piece of it was stuck in the screen."

"I wish we had the whole thing, but this is a lot. We can take it to Luke."

"Or, you can show it to me now." Ally jumped again at the sound of a voice behind her. She turned to see Luke in the doorway of the bedroom.

"Luke? What are you doing here?"

"What am I doing here?" He held out his hand for the piece of paper. Charlotte handed it over to him. "I was wondering what you're doing here. I overheard a call to the station from the next door neighbor that someone was lurking around a vacant apartment. When I heard the address I suspected it might be you two, so I told the patrol officer I would check it out for him, and here I am." He glanced down at the note in his hand. "This does seem pretty threatening, but we're not going to be able to use it."

"What? Why not?" Ally asked. "It has to show

motive."

"It might, if this apartment was still rented to Gary. It's not. That's why it's empty. He broke his lease and moved out. Which means anyone could have been in here, and anyone could have left that note. Besides that, we don't have the whole thing."

"You don't think you can find Gary's fingerprints on it?" Charlotte peered at the note.

"No, I don't. Even if we did, it wouldn't be enough. Maybe it's from his diary, maybe it's from something unrelated to Emma. Even if we could prove that it was about Emma, that doesn't mean that her death wasn't an accident. Did you find anything else?" He met Ally's eyes. "Since I'm sure you've scoured the place."

"I haven't checked the bathroom, yet. Or the closet." Ally walked towards it, but Luke stepped in front of it.

"Let me. At least I can't be arrested for being here."

"Good point." Ally smiled at him as he opened

the door to the closet. Bare wire hangers hung from the metal pole stretched across the closet. Layers of dust covered the closet floor.

"Nothing here." Luke shook his head.

"Wait, what's that?" Ally pointed to a small shelf on the side wall of the closet. "It seems out of place here. Anything to it?"

Luke looked at the shelf. "Nothing but dust." He started to pull his hand away, then stopped. "Hm, something's not right." He pulled a glove out of his pocket, he put it on and tugged on the shelf and it came right off the wall. Behind it was a small hole in the closet about the width of the shelf. He reached inside and pulled out a stack of photographs.

"Well, now this is interesting." He held them carefully with one hand and thumbed through them with the gloved hand. "It looks to me like Gary had quite an obsession."

"That's Emma and Jack." Ally stared at the pictures.

"Some are. But there's at least ten here of Jack by himself."

"Why would he be taking pictures of Jack?" Charlotte squinted at the pictures.

"I don't know, but these aren't average pictures. They're all different locations. It looks like he might have been following Jack."

"Well, maybe he was jealous of Jack? Maybe he was still holding a candle for Emma?" Ally pointed to a picture that Luke held. "Look at that one of Emma by herself. Where is she?"

"It looks like that mall right inside city limits. It's fairly new. That means he took at least some of these photographs in the past year," Luke said.

"She looks so sad." Ally frowned. "I wonder if there was trouble between her and Jack."

"Maybe. Or maybe she sensed that someone was watching her." Charlotte sighed.

"I'm going to take this into the station. Between this and the note we might be able to get some traction on getting an official investigation started. But I can't make any promises."

"Thank you," Ally said.

"In the meantime, don't break into anywhere else, okay?" He looked into her eyes. "I don't want to see anything happen to you, Ally." He glanced over at Charlotte. "To either of you."

"Don't worry, Luke." Charlotte patted his shoulder. "We'll be more careful."

"Technically we didn't break in." Ally smiled. "The door was open."

Luke glanced over at her and quirked an eyebrow. "Are we going to bicker over forced entry?"

"No." She smiled at him. "Not at all. Thank you, Luke."

"I'm going to see if I can figure out where Gary went," Ally said to her grandmother as they left Gary's apartment. "He's on the run, and I don't want to lose track of him before we figure out just how he was involved."

"Good idea," Charlotte said.

On the walk to the car Ally thought about how lucky she was to have people to turn to when she had a problem. Maybe Emma wouldn't be dead if she had that support. Gary. Was he the murderer? Was she scared of him?

"Are you okay, Ally? You're quiet." Charlotte opened the door to the passenger side of the car.

"Just thinking that I'm so lucky to have you, Mee-Maw. You always listen to me when I have trouble with something and give me the best advice."

"I don't know if I believe that." She chuckled. "If you listened to my advice you'd have Luke locked up in a tower somewhere to make sure he doesn't wander away."

"Mee-Maw!"

"You're the one that said I give great advice." She grinned.

Ally smiled in return.

"We'll see, Mee-Maw. I just want to take things slow."

"That's just fine, it's your choice. I wouldn't want to pressure you into anything you're not ready for. What comes next for the two of you is something that only you can decide."

"Mee-Maw, I just don't..." She slammed on the brakes and gasped. Right in the middle of the road that led past the cottage and towards her grandmother's apartment complex Mavis was standing. Ally stuck her head out the window. "Are you nuts? I could have killed you!"

"Pedestrians have the right of way. Maybe you should be paying more attention to your driving." The woman continued to stand in the middle of the road with her hands on her hips. "Maybe you should pay more attention to a lot of things!"

"That's it, I'm going to find out once and for all what this woman has against me." Ally started to turn the car off.

"Ally don't. It's not worth engaging with her. She might have mixed up her medications or something. I'll call to have someone check on her. Let me see if she is okay." Charlotte rolled down her window. "Are you okay? Do you need some help?"

"Ha! Like I'd take help from the likes of you. I think not!" She turned and stalked across the street to her house. Ally shook her head as she looked over at her grandmother.

"She really scared me. Why would anyone jump in front of a car like that?"

"I don't know, but you should be more cautious around her. Something is not right."

"I agree." Ally started to drive down the road again. She glanced in the direction of Mavis' house with a deep frown. "I hope she doesn't do that to anyone else."

"Maybe we should mention it to Luke so he can have someone from senior services check in on her. There are assisted living apartments at Freely Lakes, she'd probably be much happier there."

"I don't think that woman even knows what happy is." Ally continued towards Freely Lakes.

Chapter Ten

Ally turned down the street that led to her grandmother's apartment complex. "Okay, let's see if your key is missing." She parked and followed her grandmother up to her apartment.

"I hope it isn't."

"Be careful, Mee-Maw." Ally lingered close to her as she used the spare key on Ally's keyring to unlock the door. "We still don't know why the shop was broken into."

"Ally, really, you don't have to hover over me like this. I'm sure whatever happened in the shop was just a mix-up. No one is after us in particular."

"No, maybe not, but it's better to be safe. Besides, if I was really hovering I would ask Luke to give you an officer escort."

"Ally, you'd better not! That would be awful, and embarrassing!" She opened her door and stepped inside with Ally right behind her. When

Charlotte flipped the light switch the living room was revealed to them both. The couch was overturned, the end tables were strewn across the room and every drawer had been emptied onto the floor. Charlotte gasped as Ally grabbed her grandmother's arm.

"Someone could still be in here. Come back outside." She gave her grandmother's arm a tug.

"All of my things!" Charlotte groaned. "How am I ever going to clean up this mess?" She pulled away from Ally and began picking things up off the floor.

"Mee-Maw, please, don't clean anything up. Let me call Luke and have him come over here to check things out." She dialed his number as Charlotte stood in the middle of what appeared to be the aftermath of a tornado.

"This is why we need to live together, Mee-Maw, what if you had been home when someone broke in?"

"I think people who break in generally make sure that no one is home first." Charlotte crossed her arms.

"Mee-Maw, you know what I mean."

Luke picked up the phone. "Hi Ally."

"Luke, someone broke into Mee-Maw's apartment and ransacked it. We're here now."

"Are you sure that no one else is inside?" Luke asked quickly.

"I don't think so. We haven't heard anything. But I haven't looked through the entire place."

"Stay outside until I get there. I'm sending officers over now."

"Thank you, Luke." She hung up the phone and grabbed her grandmother's arm again. "Luke said we should wait outside, let's go."

Charlotte appeared dazed as she followed after Ally. Once outside Ally balled her hands into fists. "You shouldn't live alone, Mee-Maw, it's not safe."

"Stop that right this second, young lady. I can take care of myself just fine. There will never be a time when any criminal is able to drive me out of my home. No matter what anyone has to say I will not be giving up my apartment. Understand?"

Ally took a deep breath and nodded. "You're right. You have a right to live anywhere you want. I just can't believe this happened. First the shop, now your apartment."

"It really feels personal now." Charlotte narrowed her eyes. "I wonder what they were looking for."

Luke jogged up to them, his cheeks red as if he ran the whole way from the parking lot. "Is everyone okay?"

"Yes." Ally frowned. "It's just like at the shop. Everything is a mess."

"Let me take a look around to make sure that no one is hiding anywhere." He moved past them into the apartment. Ally slipped her hand into Charlotte's. A few minutes later Luke returned.

"No one is in there, but the bedroom is ransacked and so is the bathroom. Charlotte, do you feel up to walking around with me to see if anything is missing?"

"Of course." Ally followed behind them as Charlotte looked for her most valuable items. "All of my jewelry is still here. Even my extra money is still in the jewelry box. It's like they never even opened it."

"A jewelry box is not the best place to store extra money." Luke glanced around. "You should think about getting a safe."

"Maybe, but I don't like to live in fear. And the point is that it's still there. What kind of burglar doesn't even open the jewelry box?" Charlotte asked.

"A burglar who is looking for something in particular," Luke said.

"But what?" Ally shook her head. "What could anyone possibly be looking for at the shop or here?"

"I have no idea." Charlotte sat down on the end of the bed. "I have to tell you though, I'm starting to get worried. If someone broke into the shop, and now to my apartment, what's to stop them from going to the cottage next?"

"Oh, Mee-Maw, you don't need to worry about that."

"Actually, I think she does." Luke settled his gaze on Ally. "It's pretty clear that this is targeted now. With the first burglary I could believe that it was random and coincidence, but this is targeted. I think it would be best if we put a patrol car out in front of the cottage, and if you plan to stay here Charlotte we could put one here, too. It's probably best that you don't open the shop."

"What?" Charlotte stood up from the bed and stared at him. "No, absolutely not. I'm not going to run and hide from some classless fiend."

Luke raised an eyebrow. "So, you'd rather put yourself at risk?"

"Luke." Ally placed a hand on his arm and shook her head. Luke narrowed his eyes and looked from her to Charlotte.

"Let me tell you something, young man, I was

taking care of myself long before you piddled in your first diaper, and I certainly will not be told what to do. It's clear that whoever is doing this is not out to cause any harm to myself or Ally. If they were, then they wouldn't have broken in when we weren't at the shop and when I wasn't home. Maybe they're trying to scare us? Maybe they're looking for something? But they are not trying to hurt us."

Luke's eyes widened with every word she spoke. He shoved his hands into his pockets. "You don't know that. You can't just assume that a criminal isn't going to hurt you."

"Just like you assumed that Emma's death was an accident? Do you still think so?" Charlotte's cheeks reddened with passion as she studied him. "Luke, I like you, I really do. You're a good man and a good officer of the law, but you're too worried about what the evidence says and not concerned enough about what your gut tells you."

"Actually, I am." He glanced between the two

women. "My gut tells me that you're both in danger, and if you continue to run your own investigation it's only going to get worse. Now, you are both very capable, I know that. But I have a little more experience with criminals. Don't you think?"

Charlotte sighed and nodded. "I suppose you're right about that, Luke. I'm sorry. I'm just a little tense. Forgive an old woman?"

"I'm sorry, I don't think I can do that."

"Luke?" Ally gasped with surprise.

"There aren't any old women here." He leaned forward and kissed Charlotte's cheek. "Why don't you two have a tea at the café and I'll come and get you when the crime scene investigation is done?"

"Aw, so sweet. I've always told Ally that you're a keeper. Isn't that right, Ally?"

"Am I a keeper?" He flashed a grin in Ally's direction.

"Absolutely." Ally winked at him. Despite the seriousness of the mess that surrounded them it felt good to be a little lighthearted. "Let's go, Mee-Maw. We don't want to be in the way."

Charlotte followed Ally out of the apartment. Ally took her grandmother's hand as they walked.

"Will you stay at the cottage with me tonight?"

"Oh Ally, I don't know."

"Please?" Ally met her eyes. "I don't want you to be alone and I don't want to be alone."

"Of course, if you want me to be there." Charlotte smiled.

As they had tea at the café, Ally's mind fluctuated between figuring out who broke in, and figuring out who killed Emma. Could it be the same person? She assumed that it was, but why? Could it be because she and her grandmother were looking into Emma's death?

"If this had something to do with Emma's death and they were looking for something what do you think it could be?" Ally asked.

"The only thing I can think of is what we bought from the sale."

"The pan, keyring and wooden box was everything we bought."

"We need to look at them and see if we can work out why someone might want them," Charlotte said.

"We'll have to look at the pan when we get to the cottage. Let's look at the keyring and box now." Ally opened up her purse. She took out the keyring and looked at it.

"It's very pretty?"

"Do you think it could be worth a lot?" Ally asked. "Maybe the gemstones are real."

"Maybe, but I doubt it." Charlotte studied it.

"And the box?" Ally pulled the box out of her purse and her grandmother looked at it.

"It's lovely," Charlotte said as she turned it over. "But there's nothing in it. It's just a box with a beautiful design."

"Maybe, like the golf clubs it's Gary's and he was angry that she sold it," Ally said.

"It's possible, but then wouldn't it be easier

just to ask for it back."

"Yes, I guess so, but who knows what is going through his head," Ally said as she put the box along with the keyring back into her purse.

"Ally, do you think that we've gotten ourselves into something that we might not get out of?" Charlotte shot her a look of concern.

"As long as we are together, Mee-Maw, I don't think that there's anything that we can't get out of."

"I agree with that."

"But I do think that we should be aware of what we're dealing with."

"What is your gut telling you?"

"It's telling me that if Emma really was murdered, maybe it wasn't just an argument that got out of hand as we've considered. Maybe her murder was planned and deliberate. There could be a lot more to this crime than we first suspected. We don't know much about Emma's history. It could be someone from her past, from her present that we didn't know about, even someone she worked with at one time. We have almost nothing to go on."

"Not nothing." Charlotte shook her head. "We know that whoever did this is looking for something."

"Or maybe they just wanted to warn us, scare us off."

"Maybe," Charlotte said. "You're right though, it's not looking like a crime of passion. If all the person wanted was Emma dead there would be no reason to come after us. Don't you think?"

"So far they've struck the shop and your apartment. That feels very personal to me. Maybe we upset someone with the questions that we asked."

"Maybe."

"Like you always tell me, Mee-Maw, there's no point to worrying."

"You're right." She forced a smile. "I'm sure

we'll get to the bottom of this soon enough. Ally smiled at her and gave her a warm hug. Even though both the shop and Charlotte's apartment were in shambles, Ally really did believe what she said. She and her grandmother had always been able to figure things out.

"Ladies." Luke walked up to them as they pulled away from their embrace. "They've finished the initial search. We can't find what the motivation for the burglaries is. There must be a reason why they ransacked both the apartment and the shop, I am just not sure what that reason is. I'm going to find the connection though and take care of this."

"It must be something to do with Emma's death."

"I don't know that for sure."

"Luke. You can't be serious." Ally placed her hands on her hips. "Of course it's connected to Emma's death."

"Now wait a minute, we don't know that. Jumping to conclusions could send us right down the wrong path. Right now we have the shop and the apartment ransacked. There's nothing that connects that to Emma."

"What about the fact that Jack's room was ransacked?" As soon as the words flew out of her mouth Ally regretted them. She hadn't intended to share that information with Luke, at least not just yet.

"What do you mean?" He locked his eyes to hers.

"Oh nothing. Never mind. I do think it's connected though." She bit into her bottom lip.

"Ally? Is there something you want to tell me?" He studied her.

"No, I just got confused. You don't have to believe that it's connected, but I do."

"It was Gary, I know it." Charlotte stood up from the table. "After you spoke to him he panicked and wanted to warn us off."

"I'll look into it. All right? If it was Gary, then I will find out. I'm not going to let this go. Anyone daring enough to cross the two of you is going to face the consequences."

Ally smiled. "Thanks Luke."

He nodded. "Meanwhile, it would be best if you stayed with Ally, Charlotte. I didn't find any keys in the apartment, and you said you didn't have them earlier. Do you have a key to the cottage on that keyring, too?"

"Yes, I do." Charlotte frowned. "Where could I have left them?"

"I have a feeling that you didn't leave them anywhere. I think someone took them out of your purse."

"When?" Charlotte shook her head. "I can't think of a time when I left my purse behind."

"A skilled pickpocket can steal keys while you're standing right in front of them. Can you think of anyone you know that acted strange around you?"

"No, no one," Charlotte said thoughtfully.

"Okay, well if you think of anyone please let

me know."

"Okay. I will."

"Also, I'll be stationing a patrol car outside the cottage. I highly recommend that you keep the shop closed."

"Luke, I don't think a patrol car is really necessary." Ally shrugged. "Mee-Maw and I will be just fine."

"Ally, it'll be safer if you have someone there."

Ally's mind raced. She knew that if there was a patrol car outside the cottage Luke would be aware of her coming and going. She knew that he was trying to investigate, but he was busy with his other case and she wasn't ready to sit and wait for him to figure out the case step-by-step.

"I'd rather have that officer working on solving a crime. I understand where you're coming from, Luke, but please, let's hold off on the patrol car."

"Fine. I can't force the protection on you. But I will be coming by to check on you when I can."

"That's fine." She smiled at him. "I appreciate that."

He looked between the two women as if he might say something more, then shook his head and walked away.

"It's so sweet of him to want to protect us." Charlotte waved to him when he glanced back over his shoulder.

"Sweet yes, but I'm not in any mood to sit around the cottage. I want to find Gary, and fast, before he has a chance to get away with this."

"Let's go back to the cottage and regroup. I'm sure that Peaches and Arnold need some attention."

"I'm sure they do, too. You can give them that, while I try to find Gary."

Chapter Eleven

When Ally and Charlotte arrived at the cottage Ally braced herself. She was well aware that it could be the next place that was ransacked. She tested the door knob first and found it was locked. Then she took out her key and opened it. When she poked her head inside she was greeted by a mess, but not the mess she expected. Peaches managed to get a few of the plastic bowls knocked down off the counter and was batting them around.

"Peaches!" She sighed and picked up the bowls as her grandmother stepped in after her.

"See, she misses you." Charlotte scooped up the cat and patted her head. "Don't you, Peaches?" Peaches meowed loudly.

"I know, I know. But before I can play I have to look for Gary."

"Do you really think you can find him?"

"I'm going to find him. No matter what it

takes. I'm going to find out if he's responsible for this and if he is I'm not going to let him get away with it." Ally sat down at her computer.

"Ally, you need to consider that he might already be in another country. There's no way to tell where he went."

"There's always a way." Ally began to search through the information she already had about Gary. As she reviewed his previous addresses she noticed that one of the addresses was for an apartment complex. The apartments were in the neighboring town of Mainbry. It wasn't far, but maybe it was the best that he could do on such short notice. She pulled out her phone and called the number.

"Hello, Chester Landings, how may I help you?"

"Do you currently have any apartments available?"

"No, I'm sorry, but you can get on the waiting list."

"How long is it?"

"About four months."

"Is there any way I can speed that up?" Ally pressed the phone to her ear.

"Previous tenants get first priority. Have you ever lived here before?"

"I did, but it was with my boyfriend at the time."

"Whose name was on the lease?"

"His."

"I might be able to do something for you. Give me his name and I'll look him up."

Ally gave the woman Gary's full name and then held her breath. A few minutes later the woman returned to the line.

"Are you sure he didn't already apply? My records show him with a move-in date for today."

"Oh okay, I must have misunderstood him. Thank you." Ally hung up the phone and turned to look at her grandmother. "I found him."

"Wow, that was easy." Charlotte leaned past her to look at the computer screen. "What a rundown place."

"Too easy, don't you think?" Ally frowned. "If Gary was really trying to take off would he just move to an apartment thirty minutes away?"

"I don't think so. Also, I doubt he would have been able to move that fast. He must have planned this move before the murder. Maybe he planned the murder and the move a while ago. Maybe he wasn't running at all, and it's just a coincidence."

"Only one way to find out." Ally stood back up and grabbed her keys and purse again. "Let's go take a look at the place."

"Okay, maybe we can have a quick look around." Charlotte grabbed her purse as she spoke.

As Ally sat down in her car her phone rang. She picked it up when she saw it was Luke.

"Ally, it looks like we might be getting somewhere," Luke said as soon as she answered.

"With what?"

"The medical examiner has ruled the cause of death to be undetermined. He says that from the nature of the injuries the death might be suspicious."

"I knew it."

"Don't get ahead of yourself. They believe that the blow to her head might have been caused by a blunt object not from the fall, but nothing is conclusive yet. So, a police investigation has been opened."

"That's great," Ally said.

"Just be careful, Ally, you might be right and there might be a murderer on the loose."

"Okay, Luke."

"What was that about?" Charlotte asked after Ally had hung up. Ally explained what Luke had said.

"Looks like we were right." Charlotte smiled.

"Which gives us even more reason to go and talk to Gary." Ally started the car.

On the rest of the drive to the apartment Ally noticed that her grandmother wasn't as talkative as usual.

"What's going on, Mee-Maw? Are you deep in thought?"

"I'm just trying to put these pieces together. I keep thinking that there must be something more to all of this than what we are seeing. Why would Gary go to all the trouble of cleaning out his apartment, but leave the photographs behind?"

"Maybe he forgot that they were there? Maybe he thought no one would find them? It was a pretty clever hiding place."

"Maybe. Or maybe he didn't need them anymore, since Emma is dead."

"I had assumed he moved because he was the murderer. But it looks more like he already planned to move. It seems like a big downgrade from where he was, too. Maybe he was having money problems?"

"I would imagine so if he had to take some

ratty, old golf clubs," Charlotte said.

"All of that pressure, money problems, Emma selling the house they bought together, that could have easily made him crack and lose his temper with Emma."

"You're right. I see a thread forming. But it still doesn't explain why he came after us."

"Irrational actions don't always have an explanation. Maybe he was just angry and wanted to upset us," Ally suggested.

"Maybe."

Ally pulled into the parking lot and scanned the cars. It didn't take her long to pick out the beat up old truck that Gary drove up to the yard sale. She checked the number painted on the parking spot.

"He's in apartment 1C."

"Let's take a look," Charlotte said. They looked over the apartment numbers.

"First floor on the corner." The two women walked towards the apartment.

"Oh, look at those poor plants." Charlotte huffed. "Why would he even bother bringing them with him? He clearly didn't water them or care for them."

"Mee-Maw, the plants are the last thing I'm worried about. He's home. How are we going to get him to let us in and have a look around?"

"I don't think we should. We can come back another time when he's not home."

"I wonder if we should knock?" Ally glanced at the plants, then up to the door. "We could just ask him about Emma."

"I don't know if that's a good idea. We don't want to tip him off that we know where he is. Besides, he's not likely to be the welcoming sort. If he's the one who broke into the shop and my apartment, then he's pretty angry with us. Who knows how he would react."

Ally sighed. "You're right, I know you are. But this is just so frustrating. I want to work all of this out."

"Why don't we just go home, have some dinner, and let things sort out a bit? It's important to take a break sometimes."

"Okay." Ally stared at the apartment. She was tempted to just bang on the door and confront Gary. But that wasn't going to be very productive, she knew that. Or at least she tried to convince herself of that.

Chapter Twelve

When Ally and Charlotte arrived back at the cottage Ally tried to distract herself by playing with Peaches. She pulled around her little toy mouse and tantalized the cat into attacking. However, the fun just wasn't there for Ally. Her mind kept returning to Gary and whether or not he killed Emma. As she teased the cat with the mouse again, Arnold decided to get his nose involved. He sniffed at the mouse in the same moment that Peaches swiped her paw towards it. This resulted in a squealing and hissing contest.

"What in the world is happening in here?" Charlotte rushed out from the kitchen where she was trying to distract herself by baking. Ally scooped up the cat from the floor and held her close.

"Peaches got a little over-excited about playtime and Arnold paid the price."

"Oh look at you, poor baby." Charlotte made

kissing noises at Arnold as she crouched down in front of him. "All that squealing and there's not even a scratch. You silly pig." She kissed his nose. "The cake should be done soon."

"A cake, Mee-Maw?"

"I'm sorry, I know we don't need a cake, but I needed to bake."

"It's okay." Ally sighed. "There's never too much cake. What are we going to do about the shop?"

"Well, as much as I'd like to argue the point I think that Luke is right. If we open up the shop and there is someone after us, then we could be putting our customers in danger."

"I agree. Let's keep it closed up, at least for another day. We'll have to go in and do some clean up tomorrow anyway."

"Yes, that's for sure. Not to mention my apartment."

"I will be there to help. I promise."

"You always are, Ally, I appreciate it."

151

"I think I'm going to go for a drive."

"Where to?"

"Maybe drop in and visit Luke, so that I can get an update on the case."

"And then?"

"We can't live worrying about what is going to happen next, Mee-Maw. I have to get to the bottom of this."

"But you can't be reckless about it." Charlotte looked into her eyes. "It's not worth the risk, Ally. You are too precious to me to put yourself in danger."

"I'll be careful, Mee-Maw, I promise." Ally hugged her grandmother then looked down at Arnold. "Maybe you should take him for a walk. I know he misses his time with you. That will give Peaches some time to settle down."

"That's a good idea. I'll do just that when the cake is out of the oven."

"I'll text you when I'm on my way back, Mee-Maw."

"Be careful."

Ally heard the last two words ring through her ears as she approached her car. There was no reason to pay a visit to Luke. If he had any news about Emma's death he would have updated her. No, there was only one reason for her to get behind the wheel of her car, and it was to wait for Gary to leave his apartment. If she had told her grandmother where she was going she would try to stop her or insist on joining her and she felt that Charlotte needed a break with Arnold so she could relax. There was no point in both of them being at risk.

When Ally arrived at the apartment building she was surprised to see that Gary's truck wasn't in his parking space. Excitement rushed through her as she realized she might get the chance to look through his apartment. She climbed out of the car and approached it. In the evening light it was clear that there wasn't much to the place. Even the door knob was dirty. As she started to reach for it, she heard an engine roar. A beat up old truck had just pulled into the parking lot. Her heart raced. She was about to get caught again.

"Not this time," she muttered as she ran around the corner of the building. She flattened herself against the brick wall to hide in the shadows. She heard the door of the truck slam shut. Then the heavy footsteps that walked towards the apartment. She decided that when he went inside she would take a look through the windows of his truck. Maybe there would be something there that would indicate that he ransacked the shop and Charlotte's apartment or something that could even implicate him in Emma's murder.

Once she heard the door shut she started to head towards the truck. However, instead of reaching the truck she found herself staring right at Gary's back. She froze as he started back towards his truck. The closing door that she had heard was not from him going inside, it was from him stepping back out. Maybe he forgot something in the truck, or maybe he changed his mind about going home. Either way, all it would take for him to see her was a glance over his shoulder. She could try to run, but the commotion would alert him. What she experienced was a sudden rush of adrenaline that drove her feet forward before her mind could even make sense of what she was doing. She tapped him hard on the shoulder.

"Gary?"

He spun around so fast that she let out a sharp cry. It was followed by frightened silence as he displayed the knife he held in his hand.

"Why would you sneak up on me like that?" He glowered with fury in his eyes. Ally felt tiny in front of him as his lumbering form drew closer to her. "What do you want from me?"

She didn't think she would be able to form words without breath in her lungs, and yet they began to spill from between her lips.

"I want the truth, Gary. I want to know if you had something to do with Emma's death?"

He raised the knife a little higher and pointed it right at her. "Are you accusing me of killing my wife?"

"Ex-wife." She narrowed her eyes. "No, of course not. But do you know what happened?"

"No." He shook his head. "I would never hurt Emma."

"You didn't really hurt her did you? She just happened to fall, because there was a loose floorboard from when you worked on the stairs? Or maybe she slipped when you were arguing?"

"Never." His grip tightened on the knife. "Why are you talking to me about this?"

"Because I want the truth. Emma didn't deserve to die, and I want justice for her."

"Oh, aren't you the brave little thing?" He chuckled and shook his head. "You want to know the truth?" He put the knife back into his pocket and glared at her. "Fine, I'll tell you the truth. The truth is, Emma never should have left me. She got it in her head that I was some kind of monster, just because I have a bit of a temper. I wonder where she heard that from?"

"Maybe she just wasn't happy in the relationship anymore."

"Don't you think I know that?" He sunk his hands into his hair and tugged. "I tried but nothing I could do would make it work, I didn't know how to fix it. But what I do know is that she never should have married Jack. I mean the guy doesn't even like animals. She made a huge mistake when she married him. I tried to warn her, but she wouldn't listen to me. She accused me of being obsessed. She accused me of being a stalker."

"I think the pictures hidden in the wall in your old apartment are a pretty good sign that was true," Ally said timidly.

"Oh, you found the pictures?" He cleared his throat. "I forgot them there and then when I went back they were gone. I should have burned them."

"So, how do you explain stalking your ex-wife and her new husband? Is there something good about that?"

He groaned and turned away for a moment. When he turned back Ally thought she could see tears in his eyes.

"Yes, not that you'll believe me. But yes. I wasn't stalking her. Jack gave me this off feeling the first time I met him. He just felt like a fraud to me. He acted like he loved her, but it was too perfect and it seemed more like acting than love."

"So, you had nothing to do with her death?"

He lunged towards her so suddenly that Ally jumped back. It was like he had suddenly snapped. His cheeks were bright red as he stared hard into her eyes and coated his words with fury.

"I did not kill Emma! You're looking at the wrong husband!"

Ally's heart dropped at his words. It wasn't with fear, despite how close he was. It was with surprise. As vicious as he seemed, she believed him when he said he didn't kill his ex-wife. "What do you mean? What did you find out about Jack?"

"He's not who he says he is, for one." He clenched his jaw and took a step back from her. "He's a liar. He's never where he says he's going to be. I figured he was cheating on her. I thought if I could just get some pictures of him in the act, then she would see what a fool she was being. But I could never catch him with anyone." He frowned. "I tried. But it wasn't enough. I can't believe he killed her."

"Now, wait a minute, I saw the way you acted towards her on the day of the yard sale. You shouted at her, and threatened her. Do you really think I'm going to buy the idea that you actually cared about her?"

"You don't have to buy anything. Yes, I was frustrated with her. She was giving up everything to go be with a man that was nothing but a liar and a cheat. Why wouldn't I be angry? If she'd only listened to me, maybe she would still be alive."

Ally shifted her weight back on her heels and did her best to hold her tongue. It was very possible that he was making everything up about

Jack to deflect the attention from himself, but she had to follow it up. It was something new to look into.

"I hope you're telling me the truth, Gary, because I'm going to find out who killed Emma."

"I hope you do." He scowled at her. "Maybe Emma was a fool, but I still loved her. She was a good woman. She didn't deserve to die. If she was murdered she certainly didn't deserve it. Her death had nothing to do with me. You can believe what you want about me, but I didn't do anything to her."

He turned and walked away from her before Ally could say another word. Ally recalled the knife he had. It was small so maybe he did have it for self-defense, but the fact that he was so quick to wield it reminded her of just how out of control his temper was.

Ally didn't realize how shaken up she was until she got behind the wheel of her car. Her hands trembled as she tried to grip the steering wheel. As frightening as Gary was, a part of her, deep down, didn't believe that he had killed Emma. However, she wasn't entirely sure that she could trust her instincts.

Chapter Thirteen

On the drive back to the cottage Ally decided to see if she could look at Emma's house again. If Gary was right and Jack was not who he seemed she might be able to find evidence there.

Ally slowed down as she drove past Emma's driveway. When she saw Jack's car in the driveway she thought about waiting and seeing if he would leave, but she decided against it. Instead, she carried on driving towards the cottage. She didn't want her grandmother to worry about her and she needed to calm down a bit from her encounter with Gary.

When Ally arrived back at the cottage her attention was caught by someone running down the street away from her. She couldn't work out who the person was from the distance, but they were in a hurry. What were they running away from? She told herself that she was being paranoid. It was just someone out for a run. She shook her head and stepped out of the car.

When she opened the door to the cottage she was greeted by Arnold who nuzzled her hand.

"Mee-Maw?"

"I'm here." Charlotte walked out of the back hallway. "Ally, are you okay?" She rushed over to her. "You look frazzled."

"I'm okay." Ally forced a smile. "I just had a tense encounter with Gary."

"Gary? How?" Charlotte narrowed her eyes. "Did you go back there without me?"

"Yes. I did, I was worried that he would take off again. I was just going to have a peek inside the apartment, but I saw him and I decided to talk to him."

"What happened, sweetheart?" Charlotte steered her over to the couch to sit down. "Did he hurt you?"

"No. I just got a fright. He had a knife, I think he just took it out because I startled him."

"That's no excuse! Call Luke right this second and have this man arrested."

"No, Mee-Maw, I don't want to do that. It was a very small knife and he told me that he only pulled out the knife because he didn't know who I was. I think he might have thought I was Jack."

"Jack? Why would he be afraid of Jack? Do you think he knows that Jack knows he's the one who killed Emma?"

Ally took a deep breath and ran her hands back through her hair. "I know that we thought that Gary killed Emma, but now I'm not so sure. He told me that he only stalked Jack and Emma because he suspected Jack was cheating on her. He was trying to prove it. He was clearly still in love with her and I think he was trying to protect her."

"Which would make him come up with a crazy story like that. He killed Emma in a jealous rage. This only makes that more clear."

"I'm not sure about that to be honest. I think maybe we're overlooking something. Gary is the easy suspect, but there might be more to it than that. I think we should at least look into his story and see if it might be true."

"You mean that Jack was cheating on Emma?"

"I don't know. I don't want to believe that. But it's not that uncommon in long distance relationships, and that's what they had right? Sure they were married, but he was away the majority of the time."

"That's a good point. I don't think it could hurt to look into it that's for sure."

Ally jumped when someone pounded on the door. It was heavier than a normal knock.

"Ally! Open the door, please."

Ally's eyes widened at the sound of Luke's voice. Charlotte grimaced. "What's got him riled up?"

"I don't know." Ally opened the door to find Luke on the other side. His cheeks were flushed as he stepped into the cottage.

"I need to speak to you."

"Luke? What's wrong?"

"I'll just go check on something in the bedroom." Charlotte hurried down the hall. Ally took a step back from Luke and frowned.

"You seem upset."

"Yes, yes I am upset." He frowned and closed the door behind him. "The whole way here I tried to think of a way to explain myself, so that you would actually hear me."

"Luke, just tell me what happened."

"You didn't trust me to go talk to Gary?"

"I did. I mean, I just thought, you're busy and you might not consider it a priority."

"So, you had to go to him yourself?"

"How did you know that?"

"Because I was doing my job, I went to check in on Gary and found you in the parking lot. You drove off before I could get your attention. So, why would you go to Gary?"

Ally shrugged. "I wanted to find out the truth."

"Did you talk to him?"

"Yes, I did." She frowned. "I didn't intend to, it just kind of happened."

"Okay." He sighed. "I just don't want you putting yourself into dangerous situations. Just try to think things through."

"I didn't realize I was putting myself in a dangerous position until it was too late. Actually, I think you were right about him. I'm not convinced he killed Emma. He seemed to love her and wanted to protect her."

"Whatever you may want to believe, Ally, you can't just go talk to a potential murderer. It might end badly."

"Yes, I understand that." She smiled a little. "Lesson learned."

"I'm sorry I was so upset when I got here."

"It's all right, I'm sorry for upsetting you. I'm glad you are looking out for me."

"Good. I should probably get back to the station."

"I believe there's a kitchen that needs to be cleaned." She looked towards it.

"Wait, Ally." He caught her arm and looked into her eyes. "Can we have dinner tomorrow night?"

She stared at him with a small smile. "You want to?"

"I wouldn't be asking if I didn't." He smiled.

"Okay, sure. Want to come here?"

"If you wouldn't mind. That would be nice."

"Seven?"

"Sure." He ran his hand down her arm to her palm and took it in his. "I look forward to it."

"Me too." She rested her free hand on his chest. "I promise it won't be peanut butter and jelly."

"I wouldn't care if it was." He studied her a moment longer, then walked away. As his fingertips trailed along her palm she was tempted to pull him back.

"How did that go?" Charlotte poked her head out of the bedroom. "I didn't hear any screaming or slamming."

"Luke isn't like that." Ally laughed. "I think I could stomp on his foot and he'd just raise an eyebrow at me."

"Oh, I know, I wasn't worried about Luke. I was concerned about you."

"Mee-Maw!"

"Well, you do have a bit of a temper."

"I do not!" Ally crossed her arms. Then she bit into her bottom lip. "Okay, maybe a little one."

"Don't worry about that, honey, you get it from me, and there's nothing wrong with having some fire in your blood."

"Thanks Mee-Maw."

"So, he wasn't too upset?"

"Not really. He asked to have dinner with me tomorrow night."

"Here? I can go back to my apartment."

"No, you absolutely can't. Not until we have the murderer behind bars. There was something I hoped you might do for me though."

"Ally, why do you have your puppy dog eyes on?"

"I have no idea what you mean." Ally smiled.

"Ever since you were a little girl you had that face you would make and it would get you just about anything."

"I just thought you might like to have some fun. Maybe, at a senior square dance."

"Oh no, Ally! Anything but that! Square dancing is one thing I do not like. I am hopeless at it."

"Please, it might get us some information about the suspects. Especially Mavis. I really think there's something off about her. What if she is the one that pushed Emma down the stairs?"

Charlotte sighed and closed her eyes. "My darling, I have done many things for you, but this can't be one of them."

"Mee-Maw, you don't have to dance. Just go and chat to the ladies. See if anyone knows anything about her history or whether she might have a connection with Emma. You love talking to people."

"Ally, you're going to owe me."

"I know." Ally grinned. "Big time."

"Fine, I'll go. But on one condition."

"What's that?"

"You make that poor man something better than peanut butter and jelly. Do you want me to cook for you before I go?"

"Stop it! I can handle it."

"There's that temper again." Charlotte clucked her tongue. Ally laughed long and hard for the first time in quite some time. It was good to have that break from thinking about Emma.

Chapter Fourteen

The next morning Ally and Charlotte drove to the shop early. With the door locked they began to clean up the mess left behind from the day before.

They started with the back of the shop. They got rid of the chocolates and baked goods and raw ingredients. Then they cleaned everything in the back.

When they were finished in the back they moved to the front of the shop where the real damage was.

All of the beautiful treasures they had on the shelves were scattered across the floor. Ally picked up each piece carefully and set it back in its place.

"At least not much is broken."

"The new display case should be in by tomorrow." Charlotte swept some glass into a dust pan. "Pretty soon everything will be back to normal."

"Hopefully we'll work out what happened to Emma soon as well so we can put all of this behind us."

"I hope so." Charlotte's attention was drawn to the parking lot. "That sounds like a delivery van."

"Perfect timing," Ally said as she opened the back door. It was their chocolate, dried fruit and nut delivery so they could at least start on making fresh chocolates. After Ally signed for the delivery, Charlotte went about preparing some chocolates and Ally continued cleaning the front of the shop.

After a couple of hours Ally was finally finished cleaning and was ready to help her grandmother when she heard a knock on the large front window. She turned to see Mrs. Bing, Mrs. Cale, and Mrs. White at the window. All three women waved at her.

"We're closed, I'm sorry!" Ally walked over to the window and spoke through it.

"Who is it, Ally?"

"The ladies."

"Let's meet them on the sidewalk, it'll be a nice surprise for them. Some of the chocolates should be set."

"Okay, I'll meet you around front." Ally went through the front door. Charlotte went through the back door and met them around the front.

"We're closed, but we can't leave our favorite customers without some samples," Charlotte said as she displayed a tray of chocolates. "We had to make them fresh so there are only a couple of varieties."

"Oh, thank you," Mrs. Bing said as they all smiled.

"So, any updates on Emma?" Mrs. White selected a chocolate.

"No nothing. Luke is investigating it," Ally said.

"He's so handsome." Mrs. Bing smiled as she chewed a toffee. "You're so lucky, Ally."

"Sh, don't jinx it." Mrs. Cale snatched two

pieces of chocolate.

"Yes, I agree, I'm very lucky. So, are you ladies going to the square dance tonight?"

"Absolutely, I can't wait." Mrs. Bing grinned.

"Wonderful. You're going, too, aren't you, Mee-Maw?"

Charlotte rolled her eyes. "I suppose."

"Really? It'll be so nice to have you there with us, Charlotte." Mrs. White patted her hand. "You never come to the square dances."

"It's not my favorite."

"Well, at least you'll enjoy our company." Mrs. Cale took another piece of chocolate. "I'm sure you could use a little fun after what happened at the shop."

"And at your apartment!" Mrs. White clutched her throat. "So awful."

"It's not as terrible as it seems. Just a little clean-up required," Charlotte said.

"You're such a strong woman, Charlotte."

Mrs. White nodded.

"Have any of you seen Mavis around lately?" Ally asked.

"Oh Mavis?" Mrs. Cale shook her head. "Not recently but she is quite reclusive. Why?"

"I'm a little worried about the way she's acting. It's almost as if she's not all there."

"From what I heard she hasn't been all there for quite some time." Mrs. Bing clucked her tongue. "She really let herself go after Marley died."

"Marley?" Ally asked.

"Her husband," Mrs. Cale said. "She adored him."

"How did he die?" Ally asked.

"Old age, but rumor has it that Mavis blamed the hospital he died at. The one in Mainbry. Said it was negligence. Mavis wasn't the same after that," Mrs. White said.

"But was there anything more to it? Was anything ever proven?" Ally's eyes widened as she remembered that Emma had worked there as a nurse.

"No, nothing, just rumors," Mrs. Bing said as she grabbed another chocolate.

"We'd better get back to work, ladies. Enjoy the rest of these. We'll be back open soon, and I suppose I will be seeing you tonight," Charlotte said.

"We'll have a great time!" Mrs. Cale giggled.

"I'll teach you some new moves." Mrs. Bing clapped her hands.

Charlotte smiled and waved until the women rounded the corner, then turned to look at Ally. "You're going to owe me, so very much."

"I know, Mee-Maw, I know." Ally hid a grin.

***

After the shop was cleaned up they headed over to Charlotte's apartment to straighten her things.

"I am going to see if I can find the keys," Charlotte said as they arrived at her apartment.

"If the police didn't find them, then they're probably not here."

"I just feel so awful that it's my fault all of this happened." She sighed and put a couch cushion back on the couch.

"It's not your fault, Mee-Maw. Someone stole your keys."

"I know, but maybe if I'd been more careful."

"If you had they just would have broken in. The same thing would have happened, but there might have been damage done to the locks and doors."

"I suppose you're right."

"Mee-Maw, what did you think about Mavis blaming the hospital for her husband's death? Emma was a nurse there. Do you think Mavis blamed her? Do you think that could be enough motivation to make her kill Emma?"

"If she thought Emma had something to do with her husband dying, I think it's possible. With her state of mind it might even be likely,"

Charlotte said.

"Be careful when you ask around about her. Also, maybe you could find out if anyone else spotted Jack anywhere around town."

"Sure. Let me grab some things for tonight and we can head back to the cottage." She disappeared into the bedroom.

Ally set a vase upright then wiped a rag across the kitchen counter. Would Mavis be capable of all of this? She doubted it. But then she'd seen that the woman could get very angry.

"That's good enough for tonight, Ally. Let's go. You need to get started on preparing your meal."

"It's not as if I'm making a five course meal." Ally trailed after her and made sure that the new lock was secured on the door.

"Maybe you should. They say the way into a man's heart is through his stomach."

"Mee-Maw, I don't think that path is going to work for me. Unless he is happy with only chocolate."

"You don't need to worry about that anyway, you're already in his heart."

"I'm not so sure about that." Ally got into the car.

"You'll figure it out one day."

"I don't know if it's worth the heartbreak."

"What heartbreak?"

"When he changes his mind."

"Sweetheart, not every man is that way."

"I hope not." Ally turned into the driveway of the cottage. "I guess I'm going to find out."

Chapter Fifteen

While Charlotte dressed for the dance, Ally placed a call to Luke.

"I hope this isn't to cancel."

"No way. I can't wait to see you."

"Great. Then what can I help you with?"

"Could you see what you can find out about Jack?"

"Jack?"

"Yes. Have you looked into him?"

"A bit, I have someone looking into him further as we speak. Is there a reason you want me to look deeper?"

"I think you should look into his past a little, see if there are any red flags."

"Okay, I'll see what I can find."

"Thanks Luke, I know you're busy with other things, I appreciate it." After she hung up she skimmed through recipes to figure out what she would make. Even as she made her selection, thoughts of Emma played on her mind. She printed the recipe she chose and headed into the kitchen to take care of it. A few minutes later her grandmother emerged from the bedroom.

"I'm ready to go, I suppose."

Ally turned around to find her in a plaid shirt, and a matching cowboy hat. She swallowed back her desire to question just why she had that outfit stored in her closet.

"You look fantastic."

"You know I don't like it when you lie, Ally."

"I mean it, you look adorable."

"Ugh."

"Good luck tonight, Mee-Maw. Maybe you'll even have a little fun."

"I can't believe I'm doing this, Ally. Really, the things you talk me into. I don't even know how it happens."

"You look so cute!" Ally tapped the brim of her cowboy hat.

"You're not too old to ground you know." She wagged a finger in front of her face.

"Actually, I think I am."

"Keep thinking that and we'll see what happens." Charlotte huffed as she made her way out the door. Ally closed the door, but left it unlocked as Luke would be arriving soon. She held back her laughter for a few minutes until she was sure her grandmother was out of earshot. Then she laughed so loud that Arnold ran into the living room.

"I'm okay, Arnold, don't worry."

Ally walked into the kitchen and set about preparing dinner for Luke. As she got the chicken started in the oven she thought about what motive Mavis could have to kill Emma. Why would Mavis want to hurt her? Did she really think that Emma had something to do with her husband's death? It occurred to her that the woman might have just been confused and frightened herself. If she was beginning to lose her memory then she might not even remember committing the crime. She stirred the vegetables on the stove then slid the biscuits into the oven. As she closed the oven door she heard a knock.

"Come on in, Luke."

She heard the front door open and close. Only then did it occur to her that it might not be Luke. She could have invited just anyone inside.

"Luke?"

He stepped into the kitchen with a bottle of wine in his hand and a smile on his lips. "That smells delicious, you didn't have to go to so much trouble."

"I wanted to. Besides, it's no trouble to make this for you. Thank you for this." She took the bottle of wine and placed it on the counter. Then she set two glasses on the counter. Luke picked up the wine to open it while Ally carried some plates to the table.

"So, how was your day?"

"Don't you mean, did I find out anything about Jack?" He set the glasses on the table in front of the plates.

"I wasn't sure if you would want to talk about the investigation tonight." She carried the platter to the table.

"I find it hard to believe that you could talk about anything else." He pulled out a chair for her. She smiled as she sat down.

"You know me too well, Luke."

"Well enough to find out how you knew that Jack's bedroom was ransacked?"

"Uh, so did you find out anything about him?"

"Okay, I see." He smiled. "Actually yes, I did. I found out that he doesn't have much of a history, anywhere, that I can find. It's pretty unusual for someone to have so little of a footprint. I couldn't find personal ties to anyone. So, either he's telling the truth about not having any family, or he has a terrible personality."

"I could believe either." She served him some chicken and vegetables. He cleared his throat and picked up a fork.

"Another thing I didn't find out was just how you knew that Jack's bedroom was torn apart."

"Luke?"

"Yes?" He smiled, then tasted the chicken. "Wow, this is good. You might have to cook for me more often."

"Is that so?"

"Of course, I could cook for you, too. If you let me."

"I'd be honored." Ally smiled.

"So, about Jack."

"I think he might be hiding something."

"Like what?"

"I don't know. Just about every average person has a past right? So, where is his? If he doesn't have one, then how average can he be?"

"And most people who don't have a past, are criminals running from something," Luke said.

"Yes, see?"

"I'm going to look into it."

"That's good."

"Did I mention that dinner is amazing?"

"There's cake, too." She smiled. "Mee-Maw made it, and it is scrumptious."

"Wonderful."

After they shared a piece of cake Ally led him out onto the porch. "A little fresh air might bring us down from that sugar buzz."

"It was so good, but I couldn't eat another bite." He leaned against the porch railing. When she stood beside him he wrapped his arm around her waist.

"I'm so glad we spent some time together tonight. With everything going on, it's so easy to get caught up."

"So, tell me, what's on your mind?" He pulled her closer.

"I just keep thinking about Mavis."

"Really?"

"Yes. What if she's lost it? I heard her

husband died at the hospital where Emma worked and there are rumors that she believed the hospital was negligent. Maybe she thought Emma was involved."

"Do you really think that would be enough for her to commit murder?"

"At first, I didn't. I thought it was a little far-fetched. But if Mavis' mind is a little off-balance, maybe that was enough for her to push Emma down the stairs."

"So, first it was Gary, who might have sabotaged the stairs. Now it's Mavis, who might have killed Emma over her husband. Who else?" He trailed his fingers down across her hand.

"I don't know. Maybe Jack?"

"Jack has an alibi."

"A solid one?" Ally asked.

"As solid as it can be, he was on the road."

"So it's flimsy at best. But honestly, Mavis is the one that gets under my skin."

"That's because she is confrontational."

"It's strange that I feel threatened by an old woman." She rested her head against his shoulder and stared up at the sky.

"I don't think it's strange. She's been very aggressive with you. That's always unsettling."

"I know, but instead of wanting to help her, I keep thinking about what she might do to me. There's something about her that just strikes me as very suspicious."

"I can understand that. She's the secretive sort. However, she might be losing her memory or just be paranoid."

"I'm worried about her, too. She lives all alone in that house. No family nearby, no one to help her. That just doesn't seem right."

He chuckled beside her ear and turned his lips to kiss her cheek. "That's what I enjoy so much about you, Ally."

"What?" She pulled back to look into his eyes.

"One moment you're telling me why you're afraid of her, and the next moment you're telling me that you worry about her. You don't let judgment stop you from being kind."

"Hopefully, I'll find some evidence soon and then we'll know the truth. So, you're not going to answer the question?" He walked towards her. "About how you discovered that Jack's bedroom was ransacked?"

"Does it matter?" She held her breath as he paused right in front of her.

"I think maybe it should." His smooth tone and the gentle touch of his fingertips along her cheek soothed her even as her heart raced. "I've asked you to be careful, not because I want to tell you what to do, but because you're important to me, Ally, and I wouldn't ever want something to happen to you. But I'd much prefer you were honest with me, instead of hiding the truth."

"I might have slipped into the house to take a look around."

"Slipped?" He quirked a brow and smiled. "Like you tripped over the step and fell into the house?"

"I knew where Emma hid a key." She braced herself as she looked into his eyes. "Are you going to arrest me for breaking and entering?"

He laughed and looked away. The tension shattered between them. When he looked back at her his eyes still shimmered with amusement.

"No, Ally." He brushed his hands back through her hair and off her shoulders. Then he settled his palms on the slope of her neck. "I am not going to arrest you. Is that what you think?"

"I think you take your job very seriously and I would never want to put you in a difficult position."

"I love my job." He nodded then looked back into her eyes. "But I care about you and I don't want you to be in any danger. You shouldn't be afraid to tell me things. I want you to be honest with me. Even if that means I know you're a sneaky criminal."

"That's a little harsh." She couldn't resist a smile.

"Is it?" He drew his hands away from her shoulders and settled them on her hips instead. "Because I thought it was a pretty accurate description for someone guilty of breaking and entering."

"I had a key."

"Mmhm, I suppose we can let it slide then." His lips met hers and all of the anxiety she felt over what he might think of her was silenced by a surge of passion. Her arms slid around his waist as she held him close and continued the kiss. For just an instant she forgot about everything. Then he broke the kiss and leaned back so that he could stare into her eyes again. "I'm going to do whatever it takes to keep you safe, Ally. But you need to know that no matter what you can always tell me the truth."

"And maybe you need to consider that I can take care of myself. You don't need to protect me."

"That's where you're wrong." He shook his head. "I absolutely, one hundred percent need to protect you. I can't change that. It's just something you'll have to accept about me. Do you think you can do that?"

"I suppose I'll have to." She sighed and rolled her eyes. He laughed and kissed her again. After a quick and playful embrace they pulled apart.

"I'd better head home. I have to get up early and check out a few things. Listen, Ally." He slipped his hands into hers. "We're not always going to have the same view on things, but that doesn't mean that I don't respect your opinion. It doesn't hurt to have a different perspective, you know."

"I know." She smiled. "But when I'm right, you're going to have to admit that I was right all along."

"You can tell me you told me so as many times as you want." He gave her hand a squeeze then turned and stepped off the porch. It took every ounce of strength inside of her not to chase after him and ask him to stay. Luke always had a way of knowing the right time to go home. But sometimes she wished he wasn't so good at it.

After he drove off she stepped back into the cottage to clear the dishes from their dinner. A few minutes later the front door swung open. Ally was startled until she realized it was her grandmother.

"How did it go, Mee-Maw?"

"I'm sorry, Ally. I didn't get much information about Emma's death or Mavis. The most anyone knows about her is what I knew already and what the ladies told us which is that she's not the type to make friends or share any of her business. Even before her husband died they kept to themselves."

"Hm. So, she's been a recluse for quite some time. It's not likely the result of aging."

"No, I don't think so. I think it's more likely the result of a hard life." She plopped down on the couch and pulled off her boots. "As for the dance, I can't begin to tell you how much you owe me." Even though Charlotte sounded annoyed she smiled. Ally knew that she had a good time even though she didn't want to admit it.

"I bet you were quite popular."

"Yes, actually I was."

"Just relax, Mee-Maw, sometimes you have to let life happen. Right?" She grinned.

"Isn't it past your bedtime, young lady?" Charlotte huffed.

"I saved you a slice of cake."

"Okay, you can stay up."

Chapter Sixteen

Early the next morning Ally was at her computer. Charlotte brought her a cup of coffee.

"How is it going? "

"It's really frustrating. I keep trying to dig deeper into Jack's history, and I can't find much information about him. I've been calling his employer to confirm that he works there and all I get is an answering machine every time. He does have the proper license for driving a truck, but that's the extent of the information that I can find. If I look any deeper there's nothing there. It's as if he's never gotten into trouble, never voted, was never even born."

"I don't know why you're chasing Jack so hard. He seems like a decent guy to me."

"I don't want Gary accused of a murder he didn't commit." Ally sighed and stared down at the pattern of the rug on the floor. "I just wish I could get the pieces to fit. If I could confirm that what Gary told me about Jack was nothing but a made-up story then I'd feel more comfortable with only focusing on Gary. But it didn't seem like he made it up." She looked back over at her grandmother. "The truth is that when he looked into my eyes and told me that he didn't kill Emma, I believed him. I didn't need him to prove it, I just knew it, deep down."

Charlotte rested her hand over Ally's and nodded. "That means something, sweetheart. Let's get to the bottom of it. Maybe I can find out some information from Rose. She lives in the house next to Emma's and she always knows what's happening with her neighbors. Although she usually knows more than she likes to let on. I'll give her a call."

"Okay thanks." With Mavis not having much of a digital footprint either, Ally hit a brick wall. She brought her computer to the couch and began to search again. She was sure there had to be something out in cyberspace that would help. However, every time she tried to press a key

Peaches butted her hand with her head. Frustrated, she looked at the cat. "You want to play don't you?"

Peaches purred and rubbed her cheek along the corner of Ally's computer.

"Okay, but just for a little while." She pulled out the cat's toy mouse and began to tease her with it. Arnold, who must have remembered the toy from the last time they played, charged after it. A battle of hissing and grunting ensued that ended in the side table near the door being knocked into. Ally's purse crashed to the floor.

"Peaches! Arnold! Stop it!" Ally laughed at their antics. She stood up and walked over to her purse.

"What's all of the commotion?" Charlotte stepped out of the bedroom.

"I'm sorry, Mee-Maw, Peaches knocked my purse over. Everything's fine."

"I finished my call to Rose. I'm afraid I didn't come up with much about Jack. He was rarely home. When he was home she didn't see him much, he kept to himself. When she did try to speak to him he was very evasive. She said that he seemed secretive and private."

"Well, that is something, it means that Jack made an effort to protect his privacy." Ally bent down to pick up her purse from the floor. As she did the wooden box slid out of her purse and on to the floor. "Oh, I forgot that was in there." As she snatched it up the bottom piece of wood broke off from the top half. It crashed against the floor and something jumped out of it. "Mee-Maw, I'm so sorry it's broken." She frowned. Charlotte was too busy retrieving what fell out of the bottom half to respond.

"Look at this, look at this!" She held up a wad of money. "It was inside the bottom of the box."

"How strange. That's a lot of money, Mee-Maw."

"I know it is." Her eyes widened. "Do you think that might be what the burglaries were about? Maybe someone was looking for this box."

"I would certainly be looking for this if I lost it. Emma must not have known what was inside or she wouldn't have sold it."

"You would imagine so."

"I wonder if there's anything else hidden inside." Ally dug into the bottom of the box. Her finger swept across some paper. She pried it out of the box. "It must be more money." When she held it up for her grandmother to see they both discovered that it wasn't money at all.

"Ally, those are passports. Let me see them." Ally handed them over to her grandmother. She flipped through them. "These all have Jack's picture on them although he looks slightly different in each, with a different hair color and style. None of the passports had Jack's name on."

"So, Jack had secret identities? Why would a truck driver need false IDs?"

"A truck driver wouldn't. I have the feeling that Jack might not be a truck driver after all," Charlotte said.

Ally narrowed her eyes. "He has no friends, no family. Maybe that's because he isn't who he says he is."

"Who needs false IDs?"

"Somebody leading a double life," Ally suggested

"Maybe he's some kind of spy."

"That is a bit far-fetched, but I guess it's possible."

"Do you think this means he might have hurt Emma?" Charlotte asked.

"I think it means we need to stop looking at him so much as a widower, and start looking at him more as a suspect." Ally held out her hand for the passports. "We should start by finding out what we can about these names."

"Luke could help us with that."

Ally frowned. "I don't know about bringing Luke into this just yet."

"Why not?" Charlotte raised an eyebrow. "What do you think he'll do?"

"I think he'll arrest Jack." Ally tapped her fingertips against the passports. "Let's say he is a spy. What if Emma was killed because someone was looking for him? If we tell Luke and Jack is arrested we might be putting them both in danger."

"Okay, I see what you're saying, but I think you need to consider that Jack is probably not a spy. He might be a criminal of some kind. He could be a very dangerous man. If that's the case, he might have the means to flee before we have the chance to figure out if he was involved in Emma's death." Charlotte pursed her lips as she looked over the stack of money in her hand.

"Maybe that's his getaway fund. Maybe that's why the shop and your apartment were searched, because he was looking for that. I think we need to find out a little bit more about Jack before we turn this over to Luke."

"Aren't you worried that might upset Luke?"

"No, I'm worried about making sure that the right person pays the price for Emma's murder.

The rest can be sorted out later."

"All right, then what's our next step?" Charlotte tucked the money back into the box. "Other than finding a safe place to hide this?"

"I think we should follow him. We already know that he wasn't on the road like he claimed to be during the time of Emma's murder. Let's find out what he was doing in the city. Maybe that will give us a clue as to what he's really up to."

"I suppose we need to pay Mrs. Bing a visit then." Charlotte smiled. "We can stop by the shop and pick up some chocolates."

"Perfect." Ally nodded. "As for this box, I have the perfect place." She took a few pictures of the passports then tucked them back into the box as well. She sealed it shut, then opened the cabinet under the sink. She tore open Arnold's big bag of pig feed enough to shove her whole hand inside along with the box. After a little digging she managed to get it almost to the bottom. She doubted that any burglar would look there. "That should do it."

"Clever." Charlotte nodded. "Let's see if we can find out what that man was up to."

The two drove to the chocolate shop. Charlotte put together a sampler box and tied it with a cheery pink bow. As they left the shop to head to Mrs. Bing's house, Ally was startled when she almost walked into someone.

"Excuse me." She drew back.

"I'm sorry, Ally, I didn't mean to startle you." Mrs. Bing smiled at her. "It's just that I saw your car, and I thought maybe you were opening the shop. I felt like some chocolate."

"Well, then you're in luck." Charlotte smiled as she stepped around Ally and held out the box. "We were just about to bring these to you."

"You were?" Her eyes widened with glee. "Thank you!"

"Chocolates, for just a little bit of information." Charlotte held on to the box a moment longer and then released it into Mrs. Bing's eager hands.

"Sure, anything. What do you want to know? Pete down the street is going to have to paint his truck because his son-in-law got drunk and..."

"Nothing about Pete." Ally smiled and patted her hand. "We just need to know what Jack was up to when you said you saw him in the city the day Emma passed away."

"Oh." Her lips tightened for a moment. "Yes, I think it was him that I saw in the city."

"Did you see where he was going?"

She sighed and shook her head. "I'm not sure that I should say."

Ally's eyes widened. If Mrs. Bing wouldn't gossip about it, then it had to be something serious. "Mrs. Bing, we're trying to figure out exactly who Jack is. We believe he might have been lying to Emma. Anything that you can tell us could be helpful."

"I'm sure he was lying to her. That poor woman." She clucked her tongue.

"How are you sure?" Charlotte stepped closer

to her. "What did you see?"

"I was going to say hello to him, and ask him about the yard sale. However, before I could get to him, he met this woman at the entrance of an apartment building. She was young, blonde, and dressed far too fancy. He took her hand, and then they disappeared inside the apartment building. I'm afraid he might have been cheating on Emma."

"Mrs. Bing, did you tell Luke this?" Ally searched her eyes.

"No, I couldn't. I don't think it's right to talk about things like that with men. It might give them ideas, you know."

"Ideas?" Ally stared at her.

"Like, that if Jack could get away with it, then maybe he could, too, and since he's your boyfriend..."

"Okay, okay." Ally cleared her throat. "Enough of that. Do you remember what apartment building it was?"

"I do, it was Elm's Point."

"Thank you, Mrs. Bing, you've been very helpful." Ally smiled.

"Oh good, I'm so glad. I do like to be helpful." She clutched her box of chocolates and hurried away.

Once she was gone Ally looked over at her grandmother. "So, Jack might have had a secret life."

"A secret girlfriend." Charlotte nodded. "And that gives us another suspect. Perhaps the secret girlfriend found out that Jack was married and she decided to eliminate the competition."

"I think it's possible." Ally narrowed her eyes. "But maybe he wasn't just having an affair. Maybe the fake IDs are because he had other secret lives. Maybe he even has more than one family."

"Oh, that's terrible," Charlotte said.

"Poor Emma had no idea what he was up to. We'd better see if we can try to find this woman. I don't think we have enough to bother Luke with it."

"I don't either. Let's make sure that Mrs. Bing actually saw what she thinks she saw. She might have even confused Jack with someone else."

"Maybe. But she's pretty good at spotting people."

Chapter Seventeen

As Charlotte and Ally started off towards the city, Ally drove past Jack's house. She wanted to see if she could have a quick look inside so that she could try to find some more information about him. When they drove past his car was in the driveway. Ally thought that maybe he was never going to leave the house again.

On the rest of the drive Ally thought about how much Emma wanted to be with her husband. She was willing to sell her house and change her lifestyle just so that she could spend more time with him. In turn Jack had been cheating on her? It was a terrible thing to think. She parked in the vast parking lot of Elm's Point.

"How are we ever going to figure out who she is and which apartment she's in?"

"One step at a time, Ally. Let's head inside and see what we can find out."

"Okay, Mee-Maw. I have a picture of Jack that

I took of one of his fake passports on my phone that we can show around. If he's met her here more than once then someone might remember him."

As they walked towards the front door Ally noticed that the building had a doorman.

"Let's ask him, maybe he can help us," Charlotte said.

"Good idea. You do the talking, Mee-Maw, you're much better with people than me," Ally said as she handed her phone to Charlotte

"Excuse me, Sir, can you please tell me if you've seen this man?"

The doorman leaned close and peered at the picture of Jack on Ally's phone. "He looks familiar, but I see a lot of people come and go. Unless he's a resident here, I won't know much about him."

"Maybe you would be more familiar with a woman who he might have been meeting? Young, blonde, pretty?" Charlotte asked.

He laughed. "There are a few of those in here. Now that you mention it though, I have noticed that one of our new residents meets with quite a few people. Your guy might have been one of the people that she met with. Why are you interested?"

"We're looking into something for a friend." Ally smiled warmly at him. "We're trying to be discreet about it."

"Oh, okay. Well, you can ask her yourself, here she comes." He gestured to a woman who walked towards them with two large bags of groceries in her hands. Ally stepped in front of her with her hands held out.

"Please, let me take one of those for you."

"No thanks, I'm fine." The woman tried to step around her. Ally saw her chance to get any information disappearing.

"Wait, I was wondering if you might be able to help me with something."

"Today's my day off. Call my number and

leave a message and I'm sure we can set something up." She smiled at Ally.

"I'm afraid this is the only time I have available. Is there anything I can do?" Ally held her breath. She had no idea what she was even asking for.

She sighed and looked into Ally's eyes. "Are you failing your Spanish course in college or something?"

"Spanish?" Ally blinked. "Uh, yes, I'm really struggling."

"All right, come up with me. I can do a quick run through with you, but it'll cost extra, and this is the only time that I'll do it on my day off."

Ally smiled. "Thank you so much."

She handed Ally one of the bags. She and Charlotte followed after her into the elevator that would take them to her apartment. Ally considered telling the woman the truth, but she wanted the opportunity to look around inside her apartment.

"So, what level of Spanish are you in?" The woman led them from the elevator to one of the apartments.

"The first one."

"Really?" She paused and glanced over at Ally. "A late-in-life college student?"

Ally scrunched up her nose. "I just took a few years off."

"Oh, I see." She unlocked the door and gestured for them to follow her in. "Just set those down on the counter please. We can get started as soon as I put the frozen things away."

Ally looked around the apartment while she had the chance. If there was any doubt in her mind about the woman's profession it was erased by the assortment of language text books that adorned her shelves. Clearly she was a tutor or teacher of some kind. She didn't notice anything in the living room or kitchen that would indicate that Jack had been in the apartment for any length of time.

"Excuse me, do you mind if I use the restroom?" Charlotte smiled at the woman.

"Sure, it's down the hall on the right." She pointed to the only hallway in the apartment. Charlotte nodded to Ally before she headed down the hall. Ally knew that her grandmother would be conducting her own hunt. She glanced around for anything that would tell her the woman's name. She noticed a piece of mail on the coffee table addressed to Connie Baker.

"I'm so sorry to trouble you like this, Connie."

"Like I said, I don't mind, but you'll have to pay double. How far have you gotten in Spanish class so far?"

"Actually, I'm not here for a lesson."

"What?" She stared at Ally.

"I'm here to ask you about a man named Jack."

"Jack?" She narrowed her eyes. "Well, that's a pretty common name, but I can't think of anyone that I know personally called Jack. Is this some kind of scam? I invited you into my home, how could I be so stupid!"

"Wait, please, it's not a scam."

Charlotte stepped out of the hallway in time to see Connie pull out her cell phone. "I'm calling the police right now."

"Hold on, we're just here because a friend of ours recently died. We believe she might have been murdered. If you don't want to help, that's fine. But this is no scam," Ally said.

"Murdered?" Connie dropped the phone on the counter. "Why do you think I can help?"

"This is the man we're asking about." Ally held out her cell phone with Jack's picture on it. "Are you sure that you haven't seen him?"

"That's not Jack. That's Philip." She looked up from the picture and into Ally's eyes. "I've been teaching him Mandarin."

"Philip," Ally said. "That was the name on one of the passports."

"Wait a minute, are you saying that I've been

working with a murderer?"

"We don't know that for sure yet." Ally frowned. "We do know that he lied about where he was when his wife died."

"He's married?" Connie winced. "He told me he was single. That he traveled all over the world for business, and that was why he needed the lessons."

"He was definitely not single." Charlotte put her phone away and glanced back at the woman. "Did he tell you anything else about his work or where he was traveling?"

"No, I'm afraid not. We didn't talk that much. He would show up right before it was time for his class, and leave right on time as well. He always paid cash. You think he killed his wife?"

"We're not certain." Ally jotted her phone number down on a piece of paper and handed it to her. "Please call me if you think of anything else that he might have mentioned."

"Sure, I will. But he really doesn't strike me as

the type of guy who would kill someone. Honestly, I get a lot of businessmen as clients, and they can be rather abrasive. Philip was always polite and quite kind."

"But also attending your classes under an alias." Charlotte quirked a brow. "If you see him don't hesitate to contact us."

"Should I be afraid of him?" She looked between the two women. "Are the police looking for him?"

"Not just yet." Ally sighed. "I'm afraid we're really getting ahead of ourselves. Just be cautious. I wouldn't teach him any more classes right now."

"I don't intend to. Thank you for the warning."

"We'll get out of your hair." Charlotte gestured towards the door.

"Thanks for the information, Connie." Ally pulled the door closed behind her. The pair rode the elevator down to the lobby and hurried past the doorman.

"What a nice woman, don't you think?" Charlotte looked over at Ally as she drove away from the apartment building.

"Yes, she did seem nice enough." Ally stared hard through the windshield.

"What is it? I know that look." Charlotte tilted her head to the side and studied her granddaughter.

"I just don't understand why he would be learning a new language. He lied to Emma and told her that he was on a trip for work, and yet he was in the city learning Mandarin."

"Maybe he needs a new language for work. We did consider that he might be a spy. If he is then we might need to tread more cautiously."

When Ally pulled into the driveway, Luke's car was parked in front of the cottage.

"Ally." He stepped out of the car just as she did.

"Luke, you look so serious, what is it?"

"I found something out about Mavis."

"What?" She walked over to him and Charlotte joined them.

"I'm only telling you this because I want you to be cautious. She spent some time in a mental hospital a long time ago. She has also had a few complaints made against her over the years because she was acting suspiciously. She does have a history of mental health problems. If she comes near you, you should let me know. She could be experiencing a psychotic break or something."

"Okay. I will."

He gave her a tight hug then kissed her cheek. "So far your hunch seems to be panning out. I have to get back to the precinct."

"Thanks, Luke"

He smiled at Charlotte then returned to the car. As Ally unlocked the door to the cottage her grandmother leaned close.

"Looks like Mavis might just be our main suspect."

Chapter Eighteen

After thinking about what she knew about Emma's death all the way through dinner and a television show she couldn't focus on, Ally threw her head back with frustration.

"We were supposed to solve this by now. I just can't make the pieces fit together."

"Just try to get some sleep tonight, Ally. The funeral is tomorrow, and we need to be there to show our support for Emma."

"Along with her killer?" Ally shook her head and wrapped her arms around her body. She was so frustrated that Emma would be laid to rest before they found out exactly what had happened.

"I know it feels horrible, Ally, but yes. We need to be there. If the killer is there we might be able to spot them if they do something suspicious."

"I hope so."

"There's still time, Ally. We'll find her

murderer."

"Yes, I know you're right." Ally stretched and yawned. "I'm going to try to get some rest, I promise."

"I think we both need some rest." Charlotte kissed her cheek and gave her a warm hug. "I'm so glad that we have each other, Ally."

After her grandmother went to bed in her room Ally made her way to the couch. Peaches jumped up and nuzzled close. Ally closed her eyes. She wanted to feel tired, and ready to go to bed. She wanted the murderer to be found before Emma's funeral. But that was impossible the funeral was tomorrow.

Ally's eyes opened in reaction to a sharp rapping sound on the living room window. Peaches raised her head sleepily, but Arnold charged into the living room. Ally stared at the dark window for a long moment. At first she thought the contorted face was some kind of ethereal figure. Then she realized it was Mavis. She had her nose squashed against the window.

She knocked again, just as loud. Ally patted Arnold's head to soothe him and proceeded cautiously to the window.

Maybe she was wrong. Maybe Mavis did have something to do with Emma's death. If she did, then she could only have one purpose for being there so late at night, to get rid of Ally who suspected her. When she reached the window, Mavis pointed to the door. Ally's heart skipped a beat. Was this what Emma experienced? Maybe Mavis came over unexpected, asked to be let in, and then found a way to get behind Emma. Was that her plan now? Ally reached for the doorknob and swallowed hard as she turned it. Sure, Mavis didn't look very intimidating, but that didn't mean she wasn't off balance enough to do her harm.

"Mavis, what are you doing here this late?"

"It's Emma's funeral tomorrow, you know?"

"Yes, of course I know. That doesn't explain why you're here. Is something wrong?"

"I can't sleep, thinking about it. Emma was so

good to my Marley I can't let this go. I really thought you were someone that I could count on. I can see now that is not true. You're just as lazy as the rest," Mavis said as she leaned on her cane.

"Lazy?" Ally stared hard at her. "I turned over every rock. I couldn't figure it out. That doesn't make me lazy."

"Every rock?" She stared back, right into Ally's eyes. "Because from where I'm sitting there's still one rock that hasn't been flipped at all. What is it? Are you afraid of him?"

"Do you mean Gary?"

"No." Mavis shook her head.

"Do you mean Jack?" Ally's chest tightened.

"Yes." Mavis sighed.

"There's nothing I can do. I couldn't find any solid proof that he's the one who did this."

"But you haven't looked properly. Have you?"

"How can I? He never leaves the house. I can't just knock on the door and ask Jack to let me search the house."

"He won't be there tomorrow, will he?" She smirked. "He'll be showing off for everyone at the funeral. He won't miss the attention. He's a widower now, women eat that up."

"Mavis!"

"I'm just saying what needs to be said. If you don't like it, don't listen."

"So, you are suggesting that I look through his place while he is at the funeral?"

"It seems like the ideal time to me. Unless you just want to let that poor girl die with no consequences for her killer."

"Mavis, we don't know for sure that Jack is the killer."

"No darling, you don't know if he is, I do." Mavis turned and walked away. Her last words pounded through Ally's mind. How could she be so certain? Was she trying to throw suspicion off herself? She had said that Emma was good to Marley, but was she just saying that to hide the truth? Ally's mind spun as Mavis' words ran through her head.

Chapter Nineteen

The next morning as Charlotte prepared to head off for the funeral, Ally had other intentions. She hadn't told her grandmother about Mavis' visit because she didn't want her to worry about what she was about to do. Ally grabbed the keys to the van, her purse, and her cell phone.

"You take my car. I'll get the van from the shop and meet you there, Mee-Maw. I want to stop at the shop and pick up some things."

"Are you sure? We can go together." Charlotte paused just inside the door. "It's getting late."

"No, it's fine, I'll just be a few minutes."

"Okay." Charlotte kissed her cheek. "I know today is going to be hard for you, Ally, but keep in mind that our show of support matters, too. Emma will have a beautiful funeral, regardless of who is there that shouldn't be."

"I know." Ally took a deep breath. "All that matters now is honoring Emma. I'll be there."

After Charlotte left, Ally grabbed some gloves and tucked them into her purse. Peaches wound her body around Ally's legs and let out a loud yowl.

"I know, I know, Peaches. I'll be careful, I promise." She stroked her hand back over the cat's fur to soothe her. Peaches ignored the soft touch and continued to wind through her legs. "I have to go, Peaches. It's the only time I can. You look after Arnold." She slipped out of the cottage and hurried down the street. There was a bit of heavy traffic as many of the local residents left to attend the funeral. Ally did her best to keep out of sight, as she didn't want anyone to suspect what she was up to. A few feet away from Emma's house, Ally's phone rang. She winced when she saw that it was Luke. How did he know what she was up to? She knew if she didn't answer he would worry.

"Hello?" She paused a good distance from the house.

"Hey. Charlotte just arrived without you. I

wanted to make sure that you didn't need a ride."

"No, I'll be there soon."

"Is everything okay, Ally? You sound a little off."

"I'm fine. I think the thought of the funeral is just getting to me."

"I understand. This is hard on everyone. We can get some lunch after the funeral if you want?"

"Yes, that sounds great. I'll see you soon, Luke." She clutched the phone a little tighter. It crossed her mind to tell him the truth about what she was up to, but the desire passed. It was just going to be a quick look around, and then she would go to the funeral.

Ally continued to walk towards the house. The closer she came to it, the more anxious she felt. Jack's car was in the driveway. Before she could react she saw Jack step out of the front door. He was almost to the car when his cell phone began to ring. The sound made Ally shudder. It was the same ringtone she'd heard in the shop the day it was ransacked. That sealed it in her mind, Jack was the one who ransacked the shop. He was the one who prowled through her grandmother's apartment. He must have been looking for the wooden box. What Ally couldn't work out was why he didn't search the cottage for it. She fought the urge to confront him. If he saw her then, she would blow the whole thing.

"I know, I told you already, I'm handling it. It won't be much longer. Just be patient." He paused and punched the side of the car. "Don't you dare threaten me. I will take care of it." He hung up the phone and shoved it into his pocket. Ally watched as he jerked the car door open. Someone made him very angry. He tore out of the driveway at high speed. Ally stared after the car to make sure it disappeared down the street.

One thing Ally was sure of, was that he was a liar, and a con artist. It didn't take much of a stretch of the mind to believe that he could be a killer as well. With limited time, she hurried around to the back door. She found the key under the flower pot, just where she had found it before. After one quick glance around she slid the key into the lock. It stuck at first, then turned. She pushed open the door.

Inside was a pile of trash bags. It startled her as the last time she was in the house things were quite tidy, except for the bedroom. When she looked around the kitchen she could see through the glass fronts of the cabinets that there were no dishes inside. When she stepped out of the kitchen and into the living room she saw several boxes lined up near the couch. Each one was labeled with a room in the house. Her heart dropped. Jack was leaving. He was moving out. Maybe he would leave as soon as the funeral was over? Could a grieving spouse really pack up an entire house so fast? Wouldn't he be more concerned about saying goodbye to his wife than to the house that he now technically owned? As strange as that was Ally knew it still wasn't enough. Maybe he just wanted to move on because he was too devastated. She headed up the stairs to check out the bedroom.

With each stair she climbed her mind went right to thoughts of Emma. What was she thinking when she climbed these stairs for the last time. Was she afraid? Did she know that someone was after her? Or was it just another day? She gripped the banister with her gloved hand until she reached the top. There she paused and took a breath. Sunlight filtered through the window beside the stairs. It reminded her that time was passing, and she couldn't linger.

Ally hurried down the hall to the master bedroom. If there was anything to hide, she guessed that Jack already packed it up. But maybe he didn't. Maybe he had left something behind. She opened the door to find the room was empty of everything but furniture. Even the bed had been stripped down to the mattress. The mess she'd found before was gone, which also meant there was very little chance that she would find anything that would prove Jack was the killer. Still, she opened the closet and searched inside.

She peeled back a loose corner of carpet and found nothing but dirt.

As she headed back towards the bathroom she heard a sound that made her freeze. She thought a door had opened. After listening for a few moments she assumed she must have heard wrong. After thinking that someone might be there she pulled out her cell phone. She set it to record, just in case. If anything were to happen to her she wanted the proof. Once she was sure the phone was recording she stepped into the bathroom and found a box of hair dye next to the sink. It wasn't used yet. There was also a razor sitting out. Did Jack, or whoever he was, intend to use that hair dye to disguise himself?

Ally opened the medicine cabinet and found that to be empty. As she stepped back out into the bedroom she had no idea where to look next. Then it struck her, the basement. Emma had said that she had found the wooden box in the basement. If he was hiding anything it was probably down there. She made her way towards the stairs.

Morning sunlight shone through the large window on the landing. Ally noticed movement out of the corner of her eye. She stood at the top of the stairs and stared down at the entrance area. Her heart raced as she noticed the shadow flicker across the tile floor. It couldn't be a piece of furniture if it was moving. It couldn't be a pet, as Emma and Jack didn't have any. Gary had Emma's cats.

As far as she knew Jack was at the funeral, so who created the shadow that stretched larger and larger across the floor? She held her breath and wondered if she should hide. However, she was afraid that if she moved a creak of the stairs would give away her presence. She didn't want to risk being discovered when she wasn't supposed to be there in the first place. Instead, she stood frozen where she was and waited. The shadow disappeared.

A moment later she heard the engine of a car as it pulled into the driveway. She saw a flash of sunlight bounce off a windshield through the front window. She swallowed hard and wondered if the shadow might have been a trick of light the entire time. Knowing that she only had mere seconds before someone opened the door she began to descend the stairs. Then she heard loud footsteps. Not from behind her, but from beyond the front door. A heavy fist pounded on the door. She froze at the bottom of the stairs. Where she stood she couldn't be seen through the window. Jack wouldn't knock would he? It had to be someone else. Whoever it was knocked again.

"Who's in there? Ally?"

She recognized Luke's voice right away. Her heart dropped. He knew that she was there. Or did he? Maybe if she was quiet enough, he would just give up and leave. He pounded again. She grimaced and reached for the door knob.

"Don't!" The voice emanated from the doorway of the small sitting room beside the entrance. It made her fingertips tremble before they could ever touch the door knob. "If you open that door, I'll have to kill you both. Is that what you want?"

Ally drew her hand back. She bit into her bottom lip to keep from screaming. A glimmer of silver revealed the unmistakable barrel of a gun. Luke was just on the other side of the door, it would take only one twist of her wrist to unlock the door, one loud scream to let him know she was inside. But he had no idea that there was a man with a gun. What if he opened the door without his weapon drawn? He'd be shot right there in front of her, and it would all be her fault. As much as she wanted his help, she couldn't risk his life to save her own. She stepped back from the door.

"Good, quiet now. Not a sound." Jack remained in the doorway and didn't step any closer. Ally stood where she was and didn't utter a word. She could tell that Luke was still outside the door as she heard his feet shuffle against the doorstep. A flurry of thoughts raced through her mind. Should she call out to him? Would he know that she was inside anyway? What would he think when he found out that she was there the whole time with the killer? She wished she'd listened to his advice, and never come back to the house. After a few more seconds she heard footsteps as he walked away. With every footstep her heart filled with dread. What would Jack do? Would he shoot her?

"Jack?"

"Sh."

"Jack, you don't have to do this."

"Quiet!"

"He's gone, it doesn't matter now."

"I know he's gone, but that doesn't mean anything to me. You think I don't know that you might have signaled him in some way? Come with me." He reached out and grabbed her arm. For the first time she let it sink in that it was indeed Jack, the very man she witnessed weep at the news of his wife's death, that was responsible for her murder. He wasn't just any man, she knew that now after discovering the money and IDs hidden in the box, he was most likely a criminal or a spy.

Since he was so eager to harm her, she guessed he was a criminal.

"This is your chance, Jack. Just let me go. I can leave and never say a word about any of this. You don't have to have two murders on your shoulders."

"Stop it!" He pulled her hard past the stairs and the sitting room. "It wasn't a murder." He shoved her into the kitchen in front of him, then reached past her to open the door to the basement. Ally grabbed the door frame as the basement stairs stretched out in front of her.

"What do you mean it wasn't a murder?" She gulped out the words in an attempt to distract him from whatever he intended to do next.

"I didn't know she was selling the house. She was going to surprise me once she had an offer. She cleaned out the basement. Since neither of us ever went down there, I stored something very important there, which she sold. None of this was supposed to happen."

"The box, with the money and IDs in it. The

one that we bought."

"Yes." He gritted his teeth. "If that fell into the wrong hands it would ruin my life. I couldn't be patient, or try to figure out where it was, I needed her to tell me flat out what she'd done with it. I asked her where it was, and I guess the way I asked frightened her. She ran from me to the stairs. I needed to know who had the box. I chased her, and when I reached for her arm she pulled away." He stared past her at the stairs. "Then she fell. I didn't even push her. She just fell. By the time she reached the bottom of the stairs, she was gone. You see, it was an accident."

"Oh, so really, you were the victim?" Ally sighed. She was trying desperately to placate the man so he wouldn't feel like he needed to kill her. "Then don't worry about any of this. You can explain what happened. We can let all of this go. It never has to be revealed."

"No, the time for that has passed. I searched the basement and bedroom for the box. You actually turned up with your grandmother while I was searching the bedroom and then I saw the box in your purse. I couldn't believe my luck. But now that's changed, I know you saw and have what was inside the box, and I can't risk that. I work for people that would tear me into tiny pieces if they knew the information fell into the wrong hands. I've been working for these men for years. They are ruthless. I'm sorry, Ally, but I have no choice."

Ally tightened her grip on the door even as she felt his hands against her back.

"That's because you're a liar."

"What?" He paused, as she hoped that he would.

"I know that's not how Emma died. She didn't just fall down the stairs, like you claim. What really happened?" He was silent as she teetered on the edge of the basement stairs. "Go on, tell me. What does it matter? You're going to kill me, too, aren't you?"

"It wasn't like that. She did run from me. She was at the top of the stairs and screaming at me. She kept saying that our lives were a lie, that she was never going to forgive me. She kept repeating that Gary was right, that he'd warned her and she hadn't listened. As if that jerk could love her more than I did. As if somehow I was worse than him." He grunted and continued with venom in his voice. "She lost her mind. She accused me of horrible things. I just wanted her to be quiet for a minute and listen, that was all. But she kept running her mouth, louder, and louder. Something just came over me. I just didn't want to hear it anymore. She had no idea what danger she had put me in, and all she wanted to do was argue about our relationship. She didn't care that I was a dead man. I tried to explain, but she just wouldn't listen. I was so angry, I just wanted her to be quiet for a second. So I shoved her and she hit her head against the wall and just sort of tumbled down the stairs. I didn't even think about her being at the top of the stairs. I didn't intend to kill her."

"But you did. She didn't pull away, and tumble down the stairs. You shoved her as hard as you could and you sent her flying into the wall and down those stairs."

"I suppose so." His voice softened. "When I saw her at the bottom of the stairs, I was relieved. Then I realized I'd let myself get in too deep with her. She was supposed to be my cover, but really I'd grown too attached. In my line of work I can't put down roots, and I should have known better. In that instant it was all over and I no longer had to worry about someone drawing the wrong kind of attention to me. I guess, I need to do the same thing with you." Ally braced herself. She knew there was no way she could resist his strength and remain upright at the top of the stairs. She had very few options and had to come up with a solution fast.

Ally expected to feel his hands shove hard against her back, but instead she felt him step away from her. Was she wrong? Was he going to let her live? But when she felt something metal pressed against her back and heard the safety being released her breath caught in her throat. He was going to shoot her instead. She braced herself for the shot. But what she heard was his cell phone ring. The sound made her jump. It was Jack's phone and it was coming from down the hall.

"Who is that?" Jack said to himself with exasperation. Ally tensed as she wondered if he would answer the phone. Would he shoot her first before answering the phone? She felt the gun that was pressed against her back being removed. "Down the stairs." He shoved her lightly as she slowly walked down the stairs. Once she was at the bottom he tied her hands behind her back and through the railing on the stairs. "I need you to show me where the box is, but I first have to go to the funeral." She heard him quickly walk back up the stairs. "Once I have the box this can all be over," he said from the top of the stairs. A moment later she was bathed in darkness as he slammed the door shut behind him. As relieved as she was that he had left, she was also terrified. She knew that he would be back. And when he did come back he would force her to get the box. After he had the box he would kill her! Would he kill Charlotte, too?

Ally desperately tried to untie her hands. Her arms ached as the rope dug into her wrists. She tried to calm down and think of ways to get free. Then she heard the door behind her swing open. She gasped as she anticipated Jack coming back. Had he changed his mind? Was he going to shoot her now? The light flicked on, and she held her breath, uncertain of what to do. She couldn't see the door from the bottom of the stairs and she could only assume it was Jack that started down the stairs.

"It's okay, Ally, it's okay." Relief flooded her as she recognized Luke's voice. It floated through her mind like a dream. Then she saw him running down the stairs. He knelt down and untied her hands. When she was free she turned into his muscular arms.

"Where's Jack?" She breathed the question against his chest.

"Don't worry about him, he's a little tied up at

the moment." He held her close and thought she detected the sound of tears in his voice. He cleared his throat and helped her back up the stairs. "Let's go, you're safe now."

"How did you know?" She looked into his eyes as he pulled away enough to let her get her own footing.

"If there's one thing I've learned about you, Ally, it's that if I tell you not to do something, you're going to do it. When you didn't show up at the funeral, and Jack was missing, too, I got very worried. A neighbor reported seeing someone enter the house, and I had no doubt in my mind that it was you."

"A neighbor, hm? Mavis?" She tightened her lips.

"Yes, Mavis. I guess she's been watching the house ever since Emma's death. She told me in no uncertain terms that I had to get here and fast. I guess she's not guilty of murder, just guilty of being a nosy neighbor."

"It's a good thing she was. If she hadn't

reported it who knows what would have happened. If you hadn't shown up..."

"Don't even think like that." He stared hard into her eyes. "I did show up, and it's over now."

"I won't." She sighed and wiped her hands across her face. "But I still don't understand how you knew I was here when I didn't answer the door?"

"I knew you had to be inside. So, when you didn't answer, I assumed there was someone in there with you and that you were in danger. I rang Jack's cell phone to try and distract him then I came in through the back. When I walked into the hallway, Jack was headed back to this door."

"He was going to shoot me." She shook her head.

"You solved Emma's murder, Ally. Now we have Jack for attacking you. The only problem is he can claim that you broke in, maybe even try for self-defense."

"He could, but he confessed to me. I put my

cell phone on record when I thought there might be someone else in the house with me. I should have his full confession."

"You're amazing." As he hugged her sirens blared through the neighborhood. "I'm going to take care of Jack being taken into custody. You stay here, all right? Don't go anywhere."

"I'm not going to go anywhere." She gritted her teeth. "I want to make sure that man is behind bars."

"Nothing is going to stop that now. I'll be right back."

Ally stared at the open basement door.

"I don't care what you're doing, I'm going in there!"

Ally smiled as she recognized her grandmother's voice.

"It's okay, let her in." The moment Luke gave his permission, Charlotte rushed to the back of the house. "Ally? Ally?"

"I'm here, Mee-Maw. I'm right here." She

opened her arms to her grandmother. Charlotte hugged her tight.

"I was so worried about you. Mavis called me, she was ranting about something. It took me forever to pin down exactly what she was saying. I came as soon as I understood."

"It's okay, Mee-Maw, everything's fine. See?" Ally smiled. "I'm not hurt."

"Why didn't you tell me this is what you planned?" She whacked Ally on the shoulder.

"Ow! I wasn't hurt." Ally scowled then smiled again. "We've got him, Mee-Maw. Jack is going away for murder, and I'm sure countless other crimes."

"Good." Charlotte sighed. "Now, maybe we can truly honor Emma."

Chapter Twenty

Luke had to fill in the paperwork for the case so he wasn't able to have lunch with Ally. However, later that afternoon Luke and Ally took Arnold for a walk. Ally felt a sense of peace that Emma's murder had been solved.

As they walked away from the cottage Luke wrapped his arm around her.

"Jack admitted to taking the keys from Charlotte's purse that first day you went to see him. He saw the wooden box in your purse and he needed it. He tried to recover it without anyone knowing. I can't believe you and your grandmother put yourselves in so much danger."

"But we're safe now."

"But guess who saved you at the end of the day?" He asked as he pulled her closer.

"You did?"

"No, Arnold and Peaches." Arnold looked up at the mention of his name.

"How?"

"It turns out that Jack not only doesn't like animals, but is a little scared of cats and a lot scared of pigs."

"Really? He's scared of animals?" Ally smiled.

"Yes, when he came to the cottage and was going to let himself in to search for the box, he heard Peaches and Arnold making a ruckus inside. He couldn't get himself to do it."

"Thank you, Arnold." She patted the pig's head.

"I must admit that I am growing more and more fond of him." Luke smiled. As they walked past Mavis' house Ally saw her standing outside. Ally waved to her and Mavis nodded her head slightly in acknowledgement. "Well, that's an improvement."

"It is, hopefully she'll let me help her if she needs it." Ally nodded. "What were the IDs for?"

"It turns out that Jack was involved in organized crime. We have the fake IDs he used, and can link him to several hits. He was a murderer before he ever killed Emma. He will be off the streets and so will several criminals connected to him. That is at least something."

She gazed back into his eyes that were filled with warmth. "It is. Even though it created more work for you?"

"Finding the truth isn't work for me. It's the entire reason I went into law enforcement. The fact that you value the truth, just like I do, that tells me that we have something strong in common." He stopped walking and turned her towards him. He brushed his hand lightly along the curve of her cheek. "One of many things, I suspect."

"I think you're right about that." She turned her cheek into his hand. "Thanks for walking with me, Luke."

"I love spending time with you." He paused and drew his hand back from her cheek.

"Me too." She grasped his hand before it could fall away and brought the back of it to her lips. She gazed into his eyes. He smiled, a slow easy smile, that melted her heart from top to bottom. How could that feeling ever grow old?

Ally tightened her grip on Luke's hand and promised herself that she would keep an open heart and an open mind.

"Come with me, Mee-Maw has made us some brownies at the cottage. In honor of Emma."

"How could I resist." He followed after her.

"Yes, and we have to thank a little pig and cat for protecting Mee-Maw and me."

"That we do." He laughed.

The End

Chocolate Pecan Brownies Recipe

Ingredients:

7 ounces butter

4 ounces bittersweet chocolate

4 ounces semisweet chocolate

3 large eggs

1 cup superfine sugar

3/4 cup all-purpose flour

3 tablespoons cocoa powder

1/2 cup pecans

2 ounces milk chocolate

2 ounces white chocolate

Preparation:

Preheat the oven to 350 degrees Fahrenheit.

Line a shallow 8 inch square baking pan with parchment paper.

Chop the butter and break the semisweet and bittersweet chocolate into a bowl. Gently melt over a low heat, preferably in a double boiler. Once melted leave the mixture aside to cool.

In a large bowl cream together eggs and superfine sugar with a mixer until light and fluffy. This should take about 5 minutes.

Gently fold the cooled butter and chocolate mixture into the egg and sugar mixture. Mix it in slowly and gently as you want it as aerated as possible.

Sift the flour and cocoa powder and then gently fold into the mixture. Do not overmix.

Chop the pecans and milk and white chocolate. Gently stir into the mixture.

Pour or spoon into the prepared tin and using a spatula smooth out the batter so it is even.

Place in the pre-heated oven. Check after 25

minutes. A skewer inserted into the center should come out with a few crumbs once cooked. If wet mixture comes out on the skewer then the brownies could be undercooked. If the mixture is wet insert the skewer in another spot in case the skewer hit a chocolate chunk which would come out wet even if the brownies are cooked.

When the brownies are ready take the pan out of the oven and leave to cool completely.

When the brownies are completely cooled cut them into 16 squares.

Enjoy!

More Cozy Mysteries by Cindy Bell

Chocolate Centered Cozy Mysteries

The Sweet Smell of Murder

A Deadly Delicious Delivery

A Bitter Sweet Murder

A Treacherous Tasty Trail

Luscious Pastry at a Lethal Party

Sage Gardens Cozy Mysteries

Birthdays Can Be Deadly

Money Can Be Deadly

Trust Can Be Deadly

Ties Can Be Deadly

Rocks Can Be Deadly

Jewelry Can Be Deadly

Numbers Can Be Deadly

Memories Can Be Deadly

Dune House Cozy Mysteries

Seaside Secrets

Boats and Bad Guys

Treasured History

Hidden Hideaways

Dodgy Dealings

Suspects and Surprises

Wendy the Wedding Planner Cozy Mysteries

Matrimony, Money and Murder

Chefs, Ceremonies and Crimes

Knives and Nuptials

Mice, Marriage and Murder

Bekki the Beautician Cozy Mysteries

Hairspray and Homicide

A Dyed Blonde and a Dead Body

Mascara and Murder

Pageant and Poison

Conditioner and a Corpse

Mistletoe, Makeup and Murder

Hairpin, Hair Dryer and Homicide

Blush, a Bride and a Body

Shampoo and a Stiff

Cosmetics, a Cruise and a Killer

Lipstick, a Long Iron and Lifeless

Camping, Concealer and Criminals

Treated and Dyed

Made in the USA
Monee, IL
10 September 2022

13704468R00144